PRAISE F[

"Mitchell pens a wild extrapolation of a post-apoca-lyptic North American Landscape by way of *The Road*, *Warhammer 40k,* and pulp westerns. *Chaindevils* is hard, grisly fare."

— LAIRD BARRON, AUTHOR OF *THE WIND BEGAN TO HOWL*

"Beneath the chainsaws, drugs, and miscreants - Mitchell has created a story about Seachers. Folk that reflect the worst and the best in us, trying to find answers to questions we're too afraid to ask."

— ADAM SMITH (EISNER AWARD-NOMINEE, *LONG WALK TO VALHALLA*)

"Gory and raucous weird fiction, *Chaindevils* is one of the most outrageous stories I've ever read. If you'd like a taste of *A Clockwork Orange* with a Southern accent, *Mad Max* on meth, and *Blood Meridian* with chain-saws, then you'll want to dive into this vivid and orig-inal desolation envisioned by Matthew Mitchell."

— IVY GRIMES, AUTHOR OF *GRIME TIME*

"Mitchell gathers the haunted cultural imagination of the Ozarks together with the bloody history of the US's internal border wars and the cultlike stature of their figureheads and squeezes until it all reaches critical mass and burns through the fabric of history into a desolate future. Meth-fueled chainsaw warriors and gilded femdom valkyries and giggling hooded cultists pursue truly shocking violence according to a logic we can only grasp the edge of. *Chaindevils* festers in the brain like an eldritch hangnail."

— MARK JASKOWSKI, AUTHOR OF
*MUTANT CIRCUIT, THE HEARTBEAT
HARVEST*

"It would be a mistake to call this tale a descent into Hell. We're already *in* Hell from the first page, the first *line*...No depravity is left unplumbed. No despair left unearned. No doom left unmanifested. You want an army of chainsaw-wielding meth-addicted cannibals? Bizarre masked and horned cultists? Jewel-encrusted monarchist warrior women? It's all here, and more besides. It takes a pure vision and a *lot* of guts to write something this balls-to-the-wall, and Matthew Mitchell has both. Who knows what new filth-encrusted hells he'll drag us to next, but I'm damn sure going to let him."

— MATT NEIL HILL, AUTHOR OF SHORT
FICTION

MATTHEW MITCHELL

WEIRD

PUNK

Copyright © 2023 by Matthew Mitchell, Artists, Weirdpunk Books

First Edition

WP-0021

Print ISBN 978-1-951658-33-5

Cover art and ornamental break by Buster Moody

Cover design by Ira Rat

Editing and internal layout/formatting by Sam Richard

Weirdpunk Books logos by Ira Rat

Weirdpunk Books

www.weirdpunkbooks.com

"*The idea of organizing a group to take the law into its own hands was not an isolated oddity. It did not suddenly burst into the minds of a few imaginative Ozarkers. Models of vigilantism had been shimmering on the horizon for a long time.*"

— HARTMAN & INGENTHRON. *BALD KNOBBERS: VIGILANTES ON THE OZARKS FRONTIER*

"*The Ozark hillfolk have often been described as the most superstitious people in America. It is true that some of them have retained certain ancient notions which have been discarded and forgotten in more progressive sections of the United States.*"

— VANCE RANDOLPH. *OZARK MAGIC AND FOLKLORE*

"*Misery loves company.*"

— PORTER WAGONER

CONTENTS

I.

FIELD OF PAIN

AT THE SOUTHERN ENTRY TO THE FIELD OF PAIN, thirty-three hired militiamen smoked and whispered. The circular crop of corn– sheared into a vast maze –was all that separated them from the township beyond. The soldiers, if you could call them that, heard the first song just before sunset. Young, foolish, and armed to the teeth, they quivered in their pre-war boots at the voices which sprang from the cornfield: A chorus of men– not boys– who sang full-throated, and with wild abandon.

"Bring us your brothers,
Your sons and your saints.
We'll carve out their throats,
And send home the haints."

The soldiers listened intently, hung on every word. They let their smokes burn to nubs and waited for the gassy bursts of chainsaws; wondered if the stories had been a hoax when no such engines were heard. There was quiet relief in that prospect, even as the song grew louder:

"Tell all their mothers
Not to stay awake;
Their boys been swall'ered

By the Field of Pain."

The militia Captain– a former Army brat called Belle – ordered the line forward. As the youngest among them, his comrades were distrustful of the boy's calculation. But to disobey an order from Belle would be to ignore the will of Chief Commando Larson, and so the troopers let their mutinous aspirations dissolve like the fading sunlight. For they had seen what became of deserters upon recapture at base, and feared Larson's barbed whips more than those that waited within the corn.

The song went on:

"Take ye this warning,

Go back to your state.

Chainsaws get thirsty,

Come give us a taste."

As the front line rustled corn stalks with their shoulders and entered the Field of Pain, all went quiet. The soldiers halted and exchanged looks of concern. Captain Belle kicked at the rifleman in front of him.

"Move it, scumsucker," he said.

"Sounds bad in there," a grenadier behind Belle replied. He was the only veteran of their lot; had fought against the Christian County cave guerillas the winter prior and lost his left eye for their victory. "Maybe we should–"

"Shut the fuck up," Captain Belle said. "Get in there," he stomped out a thin cigarette, "and smoke those fuckin' hillbillies."

Into the corn they went.

II.

THE CHAINDEVILS

JACK PACE TOOK A HIT FROM HIS HOOTER AND plucked an earwig from a rotting husk of corn. He studied the insect as it gnashed its pincers and writhed.

"Hush," he whispered.

Jack exhaled a stream of cannabis smoke at the earwig until it slowed its whirling limbs.

His long, matted hair was dark save for the shock of white that sprang from the bridge of his scalp. The beard slathered across his lower face had tangled into his locks, and gave him the appearance of some primordial hybrid.

Around him, men of similar design sat or stood in small circles. Bottles of grease were passed around silently, and the fatty liquid was poured into converted engines that once housed gasoline. A number of the men squatted over their weapons, and huffed vile fumes from liquid concoctions in plastic jars. Some simply stared out at the Field of Pain, jaws working with rage.

The Ozarkian Chaindevils, they were called.

Jack pulled a rubber cap off the jug beside him and dropped the earwig down its spout. The insect landed on a squirming heap of its brothers: Twenty or so– half-eaten and mad with hunger. He sealed the jug and placed it in his pack.

"Get yourself a good'n?" Stuey asked. He knelt beside Jack and worked a new chain belt onto his saw. The wound on his broad nose– incurred during a recent skirmish– was infected, and he stank of necrotic pus.

Jack rose and hauled the muddy pack across his shoulders. "Just 'nother bug," he replied. Still too warm for fatigues, he was naked beneath his ragged overalls. Scars and misshapen tattoos marked the entirety of his body: Symbols and sigils of his agony, both new and old. Black stars, fading sutures, poorly drawn instruments which promised pain– words like "Hatred," or "Killer" etched in flesh beside old gouges and closed bullet holes.

"Look' to me like you got yourself a real biter there," Stuey kept on. His meaty rolls of fat and muscle wobbled with titillation. "You think so, Daddy? Is he a mean little slut? Will he make 'em squeal for Baby?"

"We gon' find out," Jack said. "Them boys is yonder." He pointed: Two miles out, a sizzling haze of blue smoke drifted over the wall of corn. *Tobacco,* he thought. *Upper of the starved, drug of the weak.*

"I bet that little bitch'll tear right through their brains." Stuey licked his cracked lips, and rubbed his palms together. "Make 'em squeal real purty."

"Well," Jack ran a finger down the length of his chainsaw, "if'n it don't, we got dinner all the same."

"Hey, you fucker," Stuey said. His face blustered into a sudden, angry storm. "Baby don't eat no bugs. Baby eats the boy-meats." He squared his shoulders and bared filthy teeth. Blood bubbled from a fresh split around his mouth.

"I know it," Jack said and smiled at the idiot. It was– he realized– a *real* smile, and wondered how many of those he had left in the tank.

Stuey searched Jack's eyes with fists clenched. His troubled mind was blurry with misunderstanding. "Oh," he shouted. "You was makin' a funny. That's a good'n, Daddy." He slapped his oily denim knees, and barked. "Daddy's got jokes."

The gargantuan fool did not have any genuine smiles left to give, but Jack knew he had done his best.

"What say you give us a song, Baby?" Jack asked, then stepped into the rows of corn.

Stuey cleared his throat and braced the giant chainsaw against his thigh. He strapped the instrument to his right forearm with rusted clasps stripped from a dead boy's pack off a trail near their border.

Jack puffed the last of his hooter down to a nail-sized wedge and swallowed it hot. Cannabis was not his preferred narcotic but he was low on crystal, and the child warriors at hand did not warrant his remaining ration.

Save it, Jack, he reminded himself for the hundredth time that day.

The cold thrall of addiction would weigh him down if he was not careful: A sick game of checks and balances played by him and his Chaindevil brothers; one without end or clear winners.

Jack gripped his saw and hoisted it high above his knotted mane. He hoped the weed would get him through.

The Chaindevils rose from their huddles and took up their chainsaws likewise. Those of broken minds snapped back to the reality of an impending frolic through the maze. Night was imminent– would be painted with the stench of churning bone and the color of blood. Who among them would be lost? How many souls would falter further amid the slaughter? Perhaps the morning would bring peace to their heavy heads.

Bless us with full bellies, sore throats, and borders secured, Jack prayed. He called out to nothing. Everything. All that he knew.

"Send us your brothers," Stuey sang.

"Your sons and your saints," Jack and the Chaindevils joined in.

III.

THE DEATH OF CAPTAIN BELLE

CAPTAIN BELLE WISHED TO CRY. HIS AMMO HAVING been spent needlessly across the corn, the boy-soldier clutched his knife– his last hope.

"What's happenin', kid?" The man who spoke was somehow more horrible than legend had led Belle to expect: Hairy as an animal, black with clotted gore– eyes that breathed fire.

Sweat threatened to slide the blade free from Belle's palm. Those campfire stories passed around back at base between cock-talk had not prepared him for this: His worst nightmares of men made tangible; a walking, talking monster.

The Captain's comrades lay bleeding all around the corn field. Straddled by such men as the wretched creature before him, they screamed until blood and teeth choked out their punctured lungs. The one-eyed bomber– Belle's most fear-some warrior– was in the process of losing his scrotum. Legs and arms were ravaged from their sockets. Loathsome gashes pumped blood around the edges of flesh toiled by the Chain-devils and their serrated tools of torment.

The chainsaws were not a myth, it turned out.

There were other, more unspeakable acts on display, but

the boy Captain could not force himself to watch. A kid of only a year older than he hollered about *things* inside his ears. Belle sang a song inside his head to drown it out.

"You missin' your Mama?" Jack Pace asked him. "Betcha' wish y'all never come here. I wish't like Hell you hadn't." He spat a gobber of mucus and gore. "Ain't no place for boys with pop-guns."

Captain Belle waved his knife at the Chaindevil. He slashed an X through the air and moaned. The boy did not wish to die– not here in Missouri, so far from his home. He deserved more: The glory of war was his right. The town beyond the corn should have been easy for the taking. It was not supposed to end like this.

"You ready, kid?" Jack asked. The blade had made him irritated. "I think it's time."

Captain Belle fell to his knees. The knife dropped tip-down into the Field of Pain. He wept like the child he was and prayed to strange Gods– begged for the grace of those who wandered far from here.

"That's the spirit," Jack said. He ripped back the cord on his chainsaw and started towards the boy.

IV.

CULLING THE HERD

AFTER THEY HAD EATEN, THE CHAINDEVILS huddled close to their fires– used the shifting light to clean themselves and their trophies. Jack Pace set to greasing his saw.

"Daddy," Stuey turned to him, "you think we'll ever be allowed back in the house?" Naked, he sponged the blood from his forearms with a clump of moss. "Baby done good this time, right?"

"Sure," Jack replied. He yanked at Captain Belle's skull until the spine snapped. "You done good."

"How much longer?"

Jack laid the spinal column neatly on the grass: A coiled ivory snake, blanched of blood.

"Don't they know I's sorry?" Stuey was on the verge of tears.

A few of the men took notice. They watched the giant out of the corners of their eyes.

Jack straightened and turned to him. "They know," he said. "Not much longer. You'll be warm and free 'fore you know it. Like I say, you done real good." He bent and rummaged through his pack.

"Here," he said, and held out a wad of foil.

"No." Stuey screamed.

One of the Chaindevils, a man called Bristol, casually lifted the bowie knife from the back of his trousers. He stepped behind Stuey and pretended to shave his leg with the blade.

"Take it." Jack commanded. "You'll feel better."

"Don't wanna do this no more, Daddy." Stuey shook his wide head from side to side. "Baby don't feel good." He began to cry in earnest– took deep, sucking sobs that turned his face red.

Bristol met Jack's eyes and took another step towards Stuey. He passed the bowie to his slashing hand. Jack tried to ward him off, packed his returnal gaze with as much smolder as he could muster.

Most of the men had turned away, but those who did not– or could not– eyed the scene with sour mouths.

"Please," Jack said. "Smoke it. 'S'all I got left."

The blubbering imbecile slapped the foil from Jack's hand. "I can't," he cried.

Bristol hop-skipped the length between them, and plunged his bowie into the back of Stuey's skull. He dipped down– nimble as lightning– and scooped the last of Jack's crystal into his palm.

The giant crumpled and fell.

Bristol leapt over the body and leaned into Jack. "Better this'a'way," he said, and grabbed him by the hand. He palmed over the foil wrap and whispered: "You're a good'n, Pace. Smoke 'em while you got 'em."

Jack sat, and dragged his chainsaw through the mud to place it across his lap. A glass pipe was strapped to the plastic engine hub and he unholstered it. He plied open the tin wad, pinched off a shard of methamphetamine, and dropped it into the pipe. His rusted torch was hot against his aching palm.

Jack Pace smoked– *scorch, snap, suck, breathe*– and watched Stuey bleed out.

V.

A MUTINOUS FOOL

A TOWNSHIP COURIER CAUGHT UP WITH THE Chaindevils at high noon the following day. Sent by Her Majesty, she came out through the Northern gate on the back of an armored mule-boy. The courier pulled up beside the marching line as they weaved through the corn.

Her armor, painted black in the tradition of Taney County soldiers, bore the markings of buckshot intended for her heart. She lifted the mask plate from her helm and spoke:

"What say, y'all?"

Jack wiped soot from his eyes, looked up past the mule-boy. "Hidy," he said.

"Larson's boys: How many you get?"

"Thirty head, give or take."

"And of you'rn?"

"Two," Bristol said. He slunk up to the other side of her human steed.

It shimmied nervously. The courier gripped at the mount with her thighs.

"Dagsworth took a bullet from the bastards..." Bristol said, paused to twiddle his whiskers.

The courier looked about their lot. She searched them. Counted. "Where's the fat fool?"

"Well, I uh– had to put the Baby down myself. Lost his head. Wouldn't take no relief." He nodded to Jack. "Pace here done his best. Couldn't be helped."

She turned her head. The cowl creaked. "That so?"

A hawk chirped gayly overhead. Though the sun was occulted by an imminent storm, Jack shielded his brow to watch it glide. The dead man's singing voice still rang in his ears.

"What say, Pace?" The courier asked again.

"Stuey was a good'n," Jack answered. "But his fire went out. Had to be done."

She looked back at Bristol, at the bowie knife tucked into his trousers. "I'll file the report with her Majesty. You'll get notice when the case is closed."

"How many deductions," Bristol asked as she readied her mule-boy to leave.

"That's not for me to–"

"If'n you had to guess," he thumbed the handle of his blade. "We wanna come home. We're doing our damndest out here and y'all keep pushing it with your goddamn deductions."

Jack took a step back.

"How 'bout we just ask Her *Majesty* our own damn selves?"

"Cool it, Bristol," Jack said, his throat a dry tomb.

The courier produced a sawed-off from the saddle holster. "I'd advise y'all not to tarry with the likes of me." She held the boomer above her spiked shoulders of iron, and said: "Take heed, you bolt-fuckin' pigs."

Bristol laughed. The spiteful, carnivorous cackle of a hyena. He pulled the knife from his britches.

"The fuck're you doing–?" Jack started towards him, slapped the bowie from Bristol's hand.

The courier leveled the gun at his face. "Hush now, big'un," she cooed. "Mama don't need no help from Daddy."

Bristol moved to the backside of her mule-boy to fetch his felled knife. The beast lurched its iron-clad hindquarters and plugged both hooves into his chest. The Chaindevil spun to one side and shot out like a harpoon into the corn.

The courier leapt down from her mount. She wedged the sawed-off into a holster down her back; a leather sling tethered to an iron spine. Her plated knees clanged as she burst through the stalks and retrieved Bristol by his throat. She pulled him over to the mule-boy and said: "By the Law of Taney County, I hereby arrest your stupid ass for–"

The Chaindevil caught his breath and slammed his naked fist into her helmet. The dull snap of bones echoed against ill-tempered ore. Bristol reared back for another shot, fingers limp and broken.

She caught his fist and crushed it with her gauntlet–pushed back on his wrist until it severed beneath the flesh. He fell to his knees and she kicked his groin through the space between. Her plated shins thrashed his man parts up deep into his guts. His face turned blue and he vomited: A sludge of half cooked boy-meat and greenish cannabis silt.

"Tie this worm-dick to my saddle horn–" the courier unsheathed the pump-action blaster from behind her back " – or I'll start blowin' fuck-holes where fuck-holes don't belong."

The Chaindevils obliged.

The courier spurred her mount and made for the township. They stood back and watched Bristol get dragged away by the mule-boy. "Well," one of them said, "guess he gets to go home after all."

"Right on back to his maker," Jack replied.

VI.

HER MAJESTY'S REQUEST

Several nights on, the men feasted by their fire on a supper of young recruits: A small band of boys who had stumbled into the Field of Pain waving a white flag. Jack Pace cleaned his chainsaw and sipped hot grease from a pan. The last of Bristol's precious hash leaves were being doled out by a shit-huffer named Jim when the courier returned.

Armorless, she had slipped through the corn and into their flock without notice. Trained in the ways of the Blood Church school marms, her movements could be as subtle as they were brutal. She unfurled a scroll in silence and began to read aloud: "By her Majesty's word–"

The Chaindevils jumped from their rotten britches. Some screamed. Jack Pace was startled to his feet.

"In response to the destruction of one Stuey "The Baby" Samuels– a most valued veteran and active serviceman– every man in this here Chaindevil Platoon receives–" she arched her dark brow for effect " –two deductions."

The men groaned or wept– clawed at dirt and stamped their heels.

"We ain't take these offenses lightly, gentlemen. Y'all are gonna learn, come Hell or a cold edy."

The courier searched among their ragged heads– hawkish, and precise.

"Jack W. Pace," she said, and pointed her finger. "For aidin' and abidin' the uncon'ch'able actions of one Deacon T. Bristol– and his improper engagement of her Majesty's courier– you's hereby deduced a further ten."

Gasps among the Chaindevils. Someone spat. A wise old killer called Thin Ruby clapped him on the back; tears in his white and bloody eyes.

Never live to see the day, Jack thought. *Never comin' home.*

The courier tossed her scroll into one of their fires. It curled and hissed among the bones of dead soldier-children. Smoke lifted ink from the page– reduced the condemnation to the black ash of atmospheric sorcery.

Before her words had settled, the courier produced another roll of parchment from the folds of her nunnery garb. "Redemption," she said. "You'ns can take it, or die in this here corn." The courier then read them her Majesty's latest request: A mission.

The Chaindevils listened.

VII.
THE METH KING

RUMORS OF BUD TEMPER AND HIS COMPOUND HAD swirled among the living for two decades. Nearly every crank dealer, trade fair vendor, and small-time cook claimed to have either gotten their amphetamines from the compound, or to have worked with Bud directly. His meth– real or not– was the stuff of legend: A narcotic to achieve a state of boundless energy and unbridled fortitude. Said to give one a sense of the depths to which their depravity could reach; would make you see religion in violence and decipher the magick of chaos and sex. Perfection in powder.

Only once had Jack Pace ever believed it.

In the Spring of last year, a beautiful, wandering monk dosed him outside a cave after a skirmish with his caravan. Smitten with his skin, dared by his wandering gaze, Jack had cut his binds when his comrades turned their backs. The two snuck off and the holy man– an expat from the fallen Branson Empire– shared his powders beside a low fire.

The drug gripped him tighter than he had ever known possible. It wound him up and spun him loose like a fresh bale of razor wire. He fell upon the monk and the two writhed for hours, tilled the summer soil with their backs and knees.

"Where did you get it," Jack demanded with a fistful of golden hair. "Tell Daddy."

"Eureka," the monk said and groaned. "Oh, yes."

"From who?"

"Bud– yes, *please*– Bud Temper."

"You lying to me, boy?"

"I would never lie to you, Daddy."

Jack had turned him over to Her Majesty's Dragoons that same morning. He told them the monk might have valuable intel– hoped he would be rewarded.

He thought about the monk as they marched to Arkansas under the courier's orders; wondered if it was he who had set them on their course to Eureka. To Bud Temper and his compound of horrors.

One thing was for certain: Her Majesty of the Ozarkian Kingdom had reason to believe the drugs were real. Reason enough to send all one hundred and six of her most feared servants to steal them.

Jack knew the Ozarkian border would hold regardless of their absence during the month it would take to make the journey. Her Majesty's River Maids had taken up the Chain-devils former post in the Field of Pain, and would provide more than adequate defense with their serrated nets and gar-tooth swords. But the promise of redemption– pending their success, of course– weighed heavy on Jack's mind. With his most recent deductions looming, he found it hard to believe in the possibility of returning home– whatever that meant. If they indeed brought Bud Temper to ground– retrieved the crystal, managed to make it back and be freed of endless, violent servitude– what would that mean for the Ozarkian Kingdom? Who would take up the chainsaws and conjure nightmares in their stead?

Nothing made sense.

Not that the idea of survival was especially present; Jack Pace assumed their chances were slim to zilch.

For every now and again, word would come back of an attempted siege on the compound by Chief Commando Larson or roving bands of field pirates: Hard warnings of what came to those who dared to try and relieve Bud of his stockpile.

There were tales of a dumping pit on the grounds that housed a massive, man-eating hound. Other reports professed to have seen a demon's shadow that followed Temper's every move; horns and claws longer than those of a Bald Knob cultist.

A cookhouse foreman en route to the Kingdom asserted a yarn in which his crew had constructed a crude harem within the compound; the vilest of playrooms for the twisted experiments and machinations Bud Temper carried out in the comfort of his lodgings.

Jack knew these stories well, admired them with the vague reverence one gives certain aspirational efforts from afar– as did all the Chaindevils.

Thin Ruby, for example, had simped for a Slut Knight who worked Eureka and had intimate knowledge of the grisly goings-on within the compound. She told him there were bodies strung across the entry gate. Miles and miles of festering corpses– years upon years of the foolhardy dead. The Slut Knight claimed Bud Temper paid an extravagant sum of dope and jewels to purchase a disgraced Branson Baron her caravan kept as a slave. She said that once the former ruler had been turned over to the compound, Temper gutted the gargantuan with a broken pipe stem, crawled into the open chest cavity, and begged the Sluts to pleasure the corpse. They obliged, Thin Ruby told them with glee, for more meth than they could ever hope to snort.

As the Slut Knights boarded their wagons and charted the next venture, a field schooner full of pirates was seized and brought into the gates. Its crew– bound and ball-gagged by Temper's bounty hunters– were fresh-faced and afraid. Once allowed to speak, their Captain claimed ignorance of the compound and its wares. He begged for his God in the Grass, cried mercy, and swore to never speak of what they had seen.

Bud Temper himself emerged from his pleasure chamber. He was said to have regarded the ship with a sad smile before he sucked back on his jug of shine, spewed against the wooden hull, and ordered his hunters to set it ablaze. The crewmen who tried to disembark amid the flames were shot and killed before their feet touched ground. Blackened skeletons were all that remained of those who refused to flee.

"We try to slay a man like'at," Thin Ruby said to Jack, "and I reckon all of us will die. Nobody ever gonna hear of it. Just more bones on a line. Not too much longer till the earth has her say in this affair. Won't that just be the breeze? Me, I simply cannot wait for the day. My shit-stained face ain't gonna be nothing to nobody: A phantom of a thought of a man who never was. Can you feel it, Daddy?"

"No," he replied. "Can't say I feel anything at all."

VIII.

MURDER AMONG THE CHAINDEVILS

On the trail to Eureka– just after crossing the border into Arkansas– a Chaindevil named El Cazador began to bicker back and forth with Marcus. Marcus– a typically quiet man– was known by those who listened to have been a serial murderer in the aftermath of the Great Wars.

Disorder was typical to their lot, a known quantity, but given El Cazador's prowess with their sole remaining rifle, and the particular ways in which Marcus could make men scream, this confrontation was of grave concern to cooler heads. Three men had already perished since leaving camp in the Field of Pain. One to a band of guerillas just a few miles South, the other two– the youngest– had been given to the Bald Knob cultists at the toll booth altar just a day prior: An expected, costly expense. But the path ahead would brim with more nightmares than those they had left behind, and should sour words evolve into blades and bullets, the Chaindevils would suffer as a whole– as a *unit*.

"No eres nadie," El Cazador muttered, "te veo comer."

"You don't know what I'm capable–"

"Cállate cerdo. Te vi rechazar la vejiga. Sólo comes la mejor carne. Eres débil, amigo mío."

"I'll pop your sack with my teeth and–"

"¡Vete a la mierda!"

Though El Cazador's delivery was needlessly combative, Jack Pace had also noted Marcus' reluctance to dine on lesser cuts of their quarry. It was suspected that he had been the one burying lungsacks, stomach tubing, and sheets of skin to rot and fester behind bushes near their camps: A grave sin which bucked against the few tenants they observed.

The Chaindevils wasted not.

Regardless of these probable truths, it could be assumed that personal grievances played a hand in the unfolding drama. At one time– four years back, give or take– Marcus and El Cazador had shared tent rolls; made the strangest of bedfellows. The pair soon drifted apart, as was often the case, but the severance had appeared amicable. Until now, no harsh words were spoken between them.

"I'll show you what I can do. I'll show everyone how I eat." Marcus said. "I'll run the roots of your teeth through my ass and–"

"Sumergiré tus sesos en grasa y los chuparé como si fueran gelatina."

Whatever quarrel had transpired, the lack of methamphetamine rations surely exacerbated the issue. Two weeks on the road with little to fuel them, the Chaindevils– all of them– felt the pull and plunge of their unattended addictions.

"Enough talk," Marcus said. "I wanna hear you cry."

Jack made to step back into the recesses of their shambling ranks, to ease their tongues with the last of his cannabis, to try and stop it...

El Cazador reached out and grabbed Marcus by the base of his filthy rat tail. It tore free from the larger man's neck with a shrill ripping sound. Marcus screamed and El Cazador stuck his thornish fingernails into the roof of his opponent's open mouth. He wedged his other hand against the back of his teeth and pushed down. A loud pop signaled the unhinging of his jaw. Marcus passed out without a word and fell to the side of the trail in a heap.

"Stop him," Jack said. "He's gonna–

El Cazador pounced and began to gnaw the flesh from the prone man's face. By the time he was pulled away, Marcus was unrecognizable. Blood drizzled between El Cazador's whiskers. Held by two of his peers, he cackled with glee.

"Bye bye," he said. "Bye bye."

A Chaindevil called Brandi shook his head. He stepped on Marcus' torn throat with his waffle stompers until he was dead.

Once he had calmed down, El Cazador was let loose. Jack sat with him and smoked while the others cut and dressed the carcass for their next meal: Intestine, bladder, anus, and all.

"How you feel?" Jack said.

"Sorry," he answered. "He was not so bad." El Cazador pushed smoke through his teeth, and passed the blood-stained joint back to Jack. "Had a fat verga. Será bueno para comer."

Jack decided he would bury Marcus' penis– secretly– should it land upon his plate come supper time.

IX.

LOATHSOME OMENS

THOUGH THEY WERE DOWN TO ONE MULE-BOY– appetites had claimed the rest– and despite only a pound of wet cannabis and a few bales of tobacco left of their rations, the Chaindevils spirits were unseasonably high. There had been no more squabbles. They were but a week out from their destination. Nights were quiet. Day passed quickly.

El Cazador was first to spot the merchant tents: Through the cracked scope of his rifle he spied a line of them– canvas and cheap flannel– not two miles out from where they lingered.

"Ven y mira," he said to Jack.

Jack swallowed the sweet juices that swelled in his cheek from a goopy mixture of ground cannabis flower and molasses. He took the gun as it was offered and climbed upon the mule-boy's calloused back to get a better view. From atop his trembling mount, he watched bluish smoke rise from the tents. Men in aprons bustled about. Long hoses hung from shiny masks over their faces.

A cook house, he determined. "Don't see no ships," Jack said. "Might have a rig on the way."

"Or maybe it has just left," El Cazador said. "Maybe they will be alone for some time. Lo deber-íamos tomar"

Jack prodded the wad of chew with his tongue, smoothed it around against his back teeth, and reshaped it into a tight ball. "Ain't for me to call," he said. "Holler at Thin Ruby. See what he thinks."

El Cazador snatched back his rifle and stalked down the trail. He leaned into the Chaindevil horde, grabbed the old man by his leathered shoulder, and brought him over to Jack. "Qué opinas?" He asked him.

Thin Ruby had never learned the rifleman's tongue– one of few who had not– and so looked to Jack Pace atop the mule-boy for translation.

"They's a meth cook yonder," Jack told him. "Looks to me like a merchant's fair. No getaway rigs that I can see. Got it sit'cheeated by the trail. Figure they got somebody coming back for 'em."

Thin Ruby wrenched shut his wrinkled lids, and sniffed at the dawn wind.

"Can't say how many. I spot twenty-two," Jack said and hopped off the mule-boy's back. "For now," he added.

"I'm full of meat," Thin Ruby said. "We all are. Don't seem worth the hassle to cull no camps. How much grass we got? Why not an honest trade for the crystal? Ain't we men? Cain't we still buy our way through the shit?" He spat. "Maybe not."

"Don't know about all that," Jack regarded him carefully. "But we ain't got the wares to spare. If'n we want it, we're gonna have to take it."

El Cazador watched them.

Thin Ruby shrugged. "Well," he huffed out his whiskers, "never met a man could grab lightning without burning his hands. And Hell knows we need a storm.".

El Cazador bounced in his boots, braids flying to and fro. "Yes," he laughed, "Si."

X.

ADDITIONS TO THE PARTY

It was two days across the border when the trouble with the Bald Knob cultists began to unfold.

Once their doobies had been doused, Thin Ruby led half the Chaindevils to a thicket that lay South of the fairgrounds. Butcher's knives and axes were doled out; they set their teeth and waited for the first screams.

El Cazador took his rifle and four scouts armed with bolt bows to the West. The mule-boy followed them with sullen eyes.

Jack Pace and all the rest took the trail North where they waited in the shade of a black walnut orchard. The smell of copper, ink, and piss breached their nostrils. A sweet, familiar odor which reminded one of warmth, and orgasm– better days. Saliva flooded their crusty mouths. Anticipation flared.

Jack sat at the base of an ancient tree and thought about the things he would do: Killing was easy, the simplest of things– nothing at all, really. The slaughtered would far outweigh any future mule-boys– for so few in this land were worthy, capable of the torment– and taking slaves was considered an errand of fools. But survivors were important. *Necessary* to their cause.

Dead meth cooks tell no tales, but half-crippled remnants of a fevered slaughter? Leftover witnesses to depravity incarnate? Those who watched– limbless and deaf– as their best friends, brothers, and lovers were ripped from this life by the guttering, endless, whine of a four-foot chainsaw... Those were the ones who held onto their stories, would tell them to anyone who might listen. They returned home with nightmares embedded in their souls. Illnesses of the brain. Ghastly wounds. Scars.

Survivors were important, yes, and forcing them to watch was everything. More than tightening borders, more than keepers of corn-mazes, the Chaindevils were a tool: Monsters made to manage greater endeavors without being conscious of the fact. A wrench Her Majesty could turn with one languid claw and which kept the whole of the Ozarkian State from ever sleeping soundly again.

Unlike most of his comrades, Jack Pace knew what he was. He did not suffer the same sicknesses, idiocies, or ignorances that polluted the ranks in which he dwelt. His bloodlust was calculated, earned, *understood*. To slice a teenage boy lengthwise up the trousers– to guzzle the excrement and fluids which rained into his open mouth– to laugh in the face of the dead boy's friend, lover, or brother– to make sure they saw it, felt it, smelled it– to see his eyes go dark and faraway– to drink the horror like so much eggshell powder up his nose... *God*, Jack thought, *what else is there?*

A stirring motion at the corner of his eye pulled Jack's thoughts away from hate and pain. He rotated his head slowly, skull against bark: A Bald Knob cultist unfurled from the boughs of a tree beside him and dropped to the ground soundlessly. Behind it, another descended likewise.

Jack wanted to scream, but willed himself to stay still.

Their horns– massive black cones halfway up the sides of each skull– were adorned with tassels of brownish gauze that dribbled with fresh blood. Beneath the hooded masks, two pair of blazing white eyeballs lashed out from the darkness. Coal-stained mouths, toothless and smiling.

Jack rose from where he sat– back wedged against the walnut– and forced his gaze to the forest floor. "Marsha," he said. His voice croaked and he wondered if he had ever been this thirsty in his whole life. "Say, Marsha," he upped his volume, "we got company."

Marsha– the Chaindevil nearest to him– reached for the hacking cleaver tied behind his shoulders.

Jack shook his head at the hacker until he stopped. "Everybody:" he said, and held out his shaking arms– motioned for stillness. "Let's all just stay cool. Put your saws down."

One of the Bald Knob cultists laughed. The sound made Jack's head hurt. He thought about running, sprinting, getting as far away from them as he could possibly go–

A bolt-bowmen named Crawdad broke ranks and made for the tree-line. The Bald Knob cultists were on him in moments. Jack turned his head to see, and wished he hadn't.

"Don't," Jack said. "Don't hurt him."

One of the cultists moved away from the squirming mass of Crawdad. It slunk over to Jack's tree, and knelt beside him.

Jack stayed his breathing. Bored his eyes at a busted nut shell near his left foot. "We paid the toll," he said. "Please, stop–"

A series of cracks and stomps signaled the end of Crawdad. Jack Pace closed his eyes, listened to shuffling hands, pulling of meats, snapping bones. The Bald Knob cultist fumed at him– its fetid mouth agape. Jack heard the other cultist approach and hand something off. It giggled.

A wet protrusion nudged Jack's lips, parted them, and leaked oily drainage into the well of his bottom jaw. It's hardness rested against clenched teeth and he started to gag– tasted the bloody spinal-fluid– suckled greedily instead.

Two slick fingers landed on his shuttered eyelids, hauled them open.

"See," the cultist said.

The expected length of spine– Crawdad's, of course–dangled from Jack's mouth, held aloft by the masked fanatic before him.

"Suck," it mouthed.

Jack obliged until his gums were coated with tender bits and soapy slime; sucked until wind came through the other side and sent a cruel gust into the mushy pit-hole of a soured tooth he had meant to pull.

The cultist took its hand away from his face, and produced a hide satchel from the folds of its rags. It dipped its curled fingernail into the bag and shoveled out grayish, chunky powder.

Oh, Jack throbbed. *Give it to Daddy.*

The powdered nail plunged into the spinal hollows seductively. Then another scoop, and another, until the base of Crawdad's spine was packed with it. The second cultist reached across its partner's shoulder and unlatched a match strike ring upon its hand. It cracked the lever with its thumb and the tip popped open: A thin pink flame that shifted gradually to pumpkin orange and sulfur blues.

"Breathe," the cultist said. "Choke on it."

Jack Pace huffed his throat and pulled back as deep as his keloid laden lungs could allow. *Fuck me,* he thought, and savored the onset rush of what was surely the finest concoction of opiates, ketamine, and speed. He pissed himself and exhaled. "Let's gut them boys," he said. "Let's gut 'em, gut 'em, gut 'em, gut 'em..."

XI.

THE SAD AFFAIR OF DANDY RIGGS

A PIPESMITH– DANDY RIGGS, HE WAS CALLED– HAD wanted to attend the trade fairs for almost as long as he had been a craftsman.

The Branson Empire brought him on during the second year of service in the Third Company's horn line. A lucky break. Dandy was no good with a trumpet. He could bleat at the right pace– knew his notes well enough– but had not the passion nor temperance it took to blare a tune of war upon the battlefield. Dandy had in fact turned heel and ran in the face of the enemy on more than one occasion. He could not, he discovered, bring himself to accept destruction with a horn against his lips.

But there were other skills in Dandy's repertoire: The ability to mold and repair broken bells– with finesse and moxy– and the eventual smoothness of previously boot-crushed borings and mouthpieces which he was able to batter and scrape until they were whole again. Fortunately for Dandy, word of his prowess with a soldering gun got around to his superiors.

The Branson Empire– though not known for cruelties on the scale of Her Majesty of the Ozarks or the infidel, Chief

Commando Larson– did not suffer the shortcomings of its servicemen. Infantry might be shuffled to kitchens. Leaders could wind up churning ditches. Be it a colonel with a drinking problem, a hotdog of a rifleman, or a horn-blower scared of his own shadow... the Branson Barons offer a simple choice when roles are reassigned: Do the new, or die today.

Stood before the Council of Barons– after his particularly poor performance at the failed Panther Creek skirmish– Dandy accepted his reassignment order to the pipesmith workshop with great relief. There, he traded in his patchwork bugle for a toolbag as if it were bombs for blowjobs. He took the new, and lived. Had four years of bliss. Four *good* years.

When the Branson Empire met her end, Dandy Riggs was at the top of his game: A devout patron of the Anti-Bald Knob clergy, proud inner-wall citizen, sacrifice-taxes paid. He was made workshop lead the year prior– his predecessor had been obliterated by a heroic dose of Patriot Spice, yes, but all agreed Dandy would have succeeded him regardless.

The work was going well enough that he had been invited to his first trade fair. Dreams had been dreamt and fulfilled faster than he could process. Even had his own pipe shop off Landing Memorial– packed it to the gills with a dazzling array of screw chillums, light bulb bubblers, and hand crafted torches. All of which afforded him a healthy opium habit and a sturdy routine of fucking.

Dandy shared a cottage near Taney Dam with a busty Sheriff named Wellworth who took him for her sex pet. The couple rented chubby mule-boys and mercenaries twice a month; they traveled together to visit a hive of Slut Knights that circled their war wagons on the border of the city. Dandy and the Sheriff would gorge on anal discharge and humiliation– suffered the sweet, bloody release of as many lashings as they could afford before returning home; both of them sore backed, and in love.

Yessir, Dandy Riggs had it made for a time.

But time, she's the reaper, and Chief Commando Larson's guerilla assault on Taney Dam put an end to all good things.

One of few who survived the onslaught of automatic bolt-bows, razored whips, and hacksaw gas attacks, Dandy crawled from the blood clogged gutters of Branson with six lifetimes of tragedy and half his mind. Driven by the purest desire to be treated to anything but the kind of deaths he had witnessed, the pipesmith dragged himself beyond the burning wall. There, he made silent peace with the world beneath the body of a local brewer who had once sucked him off during border duty. Sleep came, went on for days. Nothing, everlasting.

It was the Slut Knights who saved him– found him beneath the rotted corpse on a supply raid. A redemption short-lived, once it was discovered Dandy had not escaped with his riches. Penniless as he was, Dandy had become worthless to familiar lust Goddesses made living bringers of pain.

Knowing what would become of him at the bejeweled hands of his saviors– an endless sea of brutal intercourse, the rushing tides of fatal orgasm, a further recession of coral barriers around his sea beaten sanity– he pulled a crystal hash pipe from his trousers, cradled it, hands in offerance, fine powders of supplication mashed high in the rim of its shimmering bowl– a pacifier to stave the oral hungers of this glamorous horde of half-nude battle whores.

"Mercy," he begged.

In the ensuing years, Dandy Riggs traveled with the Slut Knight caravan. Hard times. Fed little food or drug, fucked senseless at any given moment, and sore nearly all the time. Not quite among them– never far from their grasp– always leashed.

It wasn't all bad: In the iron gauntlets of his captors, Dandy created great works of art– crafted practical beauties befitting of the horde's lavish narcotic appetites: Smoking apparatuses as totems of feminine will, and pipes that whispered the soft warmth of inner thighs– the sharpness of teeth.

Dandy stoned his work with opal anal plugs, infused delicate etchings of inhuman ravagings along pipeshafts, and embedded sensuous clove-oil diffusers to secrete numbing warmth upon fleshy, sucking lips.

Beneath his captor's fiendish desire for aesthetic pleasures, he learned new skills and honed his craft. Obsession– the purest of desires– bloomed in him. He soon forgot his former life and settled into the splendors of art. Despite his bruised ballsack, Dandy Riggs positively flourished.

The day the Slut Knights showed him the merchant tent, Dandy Riggs nearly fell to his knees to give thanks to an Anti-Bald Knob God who no longer existed. He openly wept. Nothing seemed real. As if he had been restored to his former glory. As if life against the grindstone had finally split the well of hope eternal–

Two thuggish slaughter whores sandwiched him on the grass for his embarrassing display of emotion. The Slut Knights wriggled out his seed– over and over– until he was choking and recanted his joy.

The caravan dropped him off at the trade fair the following morning. They dumped his goods beside the trail, said they would return for him and their profits, and tore off again.

Dandy set up tent alone– bow-legged and weak– beside a transitory group of meth cooks and pill pressers. Happiness returned, however slowly, as he placed his wares on the grass to glitter and glow by the light of a rising star. His neighbors– a few early shoppers, early day travelers– all stopped to admire the work of Dandy Riggs. To be appraised by his peers once more– to have climbed the ranks of society, any society, even one so low as this collection of vagrant chemists and Hawkeyed opportunists– was the finest of days. The highest high.

"Hey, now," a heroin tester named Kelsey said to him. He

took off his gas mask and pointed at the trail. "This don't look too good."

Dandy watched a vast multitude of men with chainsaws descend on the tents. "Well, Hell," he said. "Ain't that just the way."

XII.

SLAUGHTER AT THE TRADE FAIR

THIN RUBY HAD A FEELING SOMETHING WAS wrong– could taste it in the air. Death hung thick in the clouds, a palpable force that stung his eyes. He motioned for his cleaver wielding comrades to follow; knew they needed to turn back and regroup with Jack Pace and El Cazador.

By the time he heard the rattle and whoops of a song, it was already too late.

Thin Ruby was old enough to remember what music sounded like before the whims of man became cluttered with handmade fiddles and obscene face-tubas; battle accouterments which came into favor after the war. He could recall synthetic beats, electric strings, and choral mutations of battery powered throats: Remnant echoes of life before the lights went out.

How strange then, for his ears to crane and be met with the pulsing cry of trap-house snares and a thudding bassline. How queer the staccato recitations of masculine urges and rapid-fire remarks on an age long gone.

Perhaps, the old man thought, *I have simply up and died.*

Reminding him that he was, in fact, still among the living, was the Bald Knob cultist he spotted near the tree-line. It held a boom-box over its horns and stomped in time to the beat. The stereo had been retrofitted with a wind-up lever– rare, expensive tech– and the masked abomination cranked it wildly. Another cultist appeared beside first, and the pair followed the Chaindevils down the hill. The harsh, sticky rhymes that blared from their speaker grew louder as they descended.

Jack Pace was at the front of the line. All tangled hair and wind-sore flesh, he reared back his saw and ripped the starter-line. Even at a distance of some measure, Thin Ruby could see unwieldy violence in his small, white eyes.

A masher named Earl leaned on his ten-foot sledge and clapped the elderly killer on his shoulder. "What say, Ruby?"

"Our boys been dosed by them Bald Knobbers yonder," he replied.

"Didn't we pay the toll? Why would they–?"

"Don't know what for. Creatures such as them cain't be put upon for answers. They been stripped of their hearts. Damned to wander stranger fields of ash than even we. Music and powders..." Thin Ruby paused, clicked his teeth. "Fire for the killing. But why, for what? Who could know the wants and needs of men bedeviled?"

"Let's get some of that dose," the masher said. "That there song they got going, boy, she pops!"

"Stay yourself, child-meat." The old man shot him a fearsome gander. "We ain't moving 'til they've sent the signal. Whatever the Hells going on over there, we don't want no part of it."

He watched the first wave of Chaindevils connect with the merchant tents. Cooks and fair-goers scattered like waved upon flies in a shit-house. Jack ran his chainsaw through the sternum of a limping pipesmith– fell upon the sputtering corpse– and cleaved him into haphazard chunks.

Once the screaming had started in earnest, El Cazador's rifle rang out across the orchard. A vendor carrying a bundle of Kratom branches disappeared in a cloud of red fog. Bolts were let loose from the bowmen: Seventy-six screeching projectiles which plunged into the scurrying crowd–wrenched heads, limbs, and torsos from all who fled beneath the torrent of chainsaws. With each passing pop and twang from the east, bodies fell in heaps, one atop the next.

The Chaindevils twirled their way into the tents–saws dancing. Gore flecked the canvas walls from within, and soaked through in bright, sudden bursts. Grease gas from converted engines billowed above, coated the heavens in sickly yellow smoke.

"That's it." Earl hauled the sledge over his shoulder. "Ain't gonna sit here wetting my britches. Going out there to have me some fun."

"No, you wretched skank!" Thin Ruby spat. "We wait for the dagnabbin' signal, or else–"

"Suckle this hog," Earl pulled at himself. He stretched on his own manhood and twisted. "Hurt me, Pappy," the masher said, and strode into the fray.

Thin Ruby watched, helpless, as the rest of the meat-dressing brigade followed. "Desperate curs," he hollered at their backs. "We ain't supposed to start yet. This ain't how we do it. Slicing up meat before it's been slit– a fool's errand, I say."

Despite his earnest protest, the old man had no choice but to take up his cleaver and trail them.

El Cazador and the bowmen advanced into the fairgrounds. They were forced to duck and dodge the passing chainsaws as Jack Pace and the other saw handlers careened by– spun out, belligerent, and bemused from the Bald Knob narcotics. Sensing a shift, an unbridled pain thirst, El Cazador plucked an infant from the arms of its pleading father. He balanced it upon the upturned muzzle of his rifle, pulled the trigger, and blew the babe apart. Hot, gummy rain showered them. El Cazador moaned in ecstasy. The childless man lashed out at him with naked fists– a barell's worth of bolts stopped him in his tracks. El Cazador jumped on his chest, stuck the barrel down his throat, and pushed down hard until something snapped in the back of his skull.

The boom-box wielding cultist stood on a pile of the wailing soon-to-be-dead. With blood moistened claws, it pinched the volume wheel, set it to blast.

Jack Pace streaked past in a blur. He chased a weeping powder foreman with a hole in his gut. The Chaindevil had a length of the man's intestine wrapped around his fist like a leash. "Gut 'em, gut 'em, gut 'em," he sang to the rhythm whooping out from the stereo.

Call it fortitude, or hard-earned wisdom– Thin Ruby knew, within moments of engagement, that there would be no prisoners today. No half-crippled escapees to hobble home and warn their families, friends, and leaders. No touring speakers, propped before nervous recruits.

Nobody would get out alive.

No witnesses.

"This is bad business," Thin Ruby muttered to himself, swung the cleaver, and watched his victim fall to ribbons.

XIII.
OUTSIDE EUREKA

TWO LONG, HARD WEEKS ON THE TRAIL LED THE
Chaindevils deeper into the Arkansas wilds. In what was typically a mild season, there had been more rain, heat, and
infighting than Jack Pace had ever known.

Sinister times.

After the massacre, drugs were aplenty, but the quality of
said goods had boiled their minds. Emotions were raw, and
suppression of cravings for violence, too thin. The Chaindevils
scratched at themselves, muttered threats to one another
without provocation. Those who were not privy to the
pregame spinal-pipe grew jealous of the privileged, while those
who had indulged– including Jack– felt the sting of with-
drawal. He also harbored a deathly guilt for having lost
control– at his inability to leave even one merchant or cook
alive. Worse than that, the slain had been so utterly desecrated
by chainsaws and bolts, there was little meat left for eating.

Between the weather, agonizing squirrel suppers, and an
overload of bad meth, a general meanness took hold in their
ranks.

As if sweltering humidity and drug-feuds were not
enough, the two Bald Knob cultists continued to follow. They

harangued various Chaindevils at random with their cruel, religious whims and dirty games. Occasionally, the cultists would climb atop some hapless bolt-bowmen to race them piggyback until they fell and could go no further. They had also crucified the mule-boy on a barren hillock– as was their custom– while no one was watching. Packs and loads got heavier in its absence, though the ones what done it suffered not.

One moonless night after they had set up camp, the masher called Earle was dragged to one of their private rituals in the trees. The Chaindevils tried to sleep against the sounds of his distant screams, and the baying of coyotes. When he returned with the cultists the next day, Earl was dazed and pale. Bizarre sigils were shaved deep into his back and his eyes lashed out in odd, opposite angles. The masher had not uttered a word since– walked nearly half a mile behind them.

Men began to disappear from the marching line, never to return, and in the span of a week, their one hundred and six became ninety-nine.

Even those who ranked high in an esoteric system of respect were not spared the indecencies: El Cazador– menacing annihilator of all who took breath in his presence– lost his toe to a rusty pair of shears for having dared beg a toot of the precious Bald Knob narcotics. He melted down a handful of his bullets by a roaring bon and dribbled molten over the wound. To everyone's surprise, the rifle-toting killer was back on his feet and on the trail come sun up– Hell and murder in the green whorls of his eyes.

Thin Ruby was losing patience with the others for keeping the vile creatures around. It seemed to him that men of their order ought not be forced to shiver in their skin-cots on account of filthy, masked zealots. He began to suspect the Bald Knob cultists were human– as human as he and the Chain-devils, at least. So why cater to their fear? Would their loins not flood upon the twirling band of a chainsaw?

Figure they'd bleed and chew, he thought, *same as me*. "So why ain't we done it?" he whispered down the line.

The old man still had not reconciled with Jack– his only port in an alley of storms– but word got around that he was attempting a coup against their loathsome escorts.

"I hear what you been saying," Jack told him. "You don't got to talk to me, but I hope you'll listen: Don't tarry with them Bald Knobbers, Ruby. It ain't for us to choose if they follow or not. Reckon they been sent by Her Majesty so it don't matter what for. And you, by God, are sharp enough to know it."

Thin Ruby stopped on the trail and stared at him. His whiskers throbbed and his cheeks were hard. "They aim to do us in," he said. "Showing up with fine powders and oppressive aggression... It ain't right. You know what they done to Earl? Harm gonna fall on all of us, we keep feeding them sorry freaks. I can hear it in the grass. If'n you cain't see a thicket for the thorns, I don't know what to do with ye."

Jack's gaze fell upon something behind the old man and he lowered his eyes. "Hush, now," he said. "Yonder they come."

"Then yonder I make my stand," Thin Ruby shouted. "Devils, begone from us. Get thee behind the muddy chute of mine asshole!"

"Here I was thinking you still had some sense." Jack spat and marched on. "If them things wanna nuzzle your busted ribs, they gonna find a way to do'er. You go making a scene, it ain't gonna be me what bails you out."

Thin Ruby stood like a rock in a river of men. They streamed past and he unwound a clasp tied to his loincloth. He slipped a wrist through the sling on his cleaver and gripped the handle. Rasping breaths tickled his ears from behind. The old man seethed with hatred as the cultists galloped lazily past him. His cleaver arm floated above his head, the remaining hand joined its twin upon the shaft and he prayed for a surge of will and power to bring both arms and blade crashing with might upon the horned scalps of his enemies–

"Empieza a hablar, puta," El Cazador called out. "Dime de donde sacaste esta mierda."

"Don't shoot," he heard Jack say. "Keep him alive, goddamnit."

The Bald Knobbers craned their crooked necks.

–Thin Ruby put his arm down, quickly lashed the cleaver back to his waist.

"Quien mierda eres tu?"

The old man nudged through to the front of the line: A circle of Chaindevils had formed in the trail, and when he managed to push past Jack– careful to avoid the cultists who also stood watching– he saw a man covered in red sludge at its center. The wretch was so coated in the stuff, he reminded him of a slick, mutant crappie he once fished from the Roiling River as a boy.

"Fuck's going on here?" Thin Ruby asked.

"Wandered onto the trail," Jack said and shrugged.

El Cazador lifted his leaden foot and kicked the man in the chest. He stumbled to the ground silently, and lay there, arms spread wide. "His eyes are wrong," El Cazador muttered. "Veo el ol-vido en ellos."

"He been dosed something fierce," Thin Ruby agreed. "Got his'self in a right sorry state. Can't feel no soul tethered to the coil. He's lost and gone to only what stars remain behind the veil. So what in Hell are y'all grilling him for?"

"Had this on him," Jack said and handed him a leather sack.

Thin Ruby spread it open and dipped his finger inside. He wiggled around and produced a bright, red crystalline hunk from the satchel. "Dear, Liza," he exclaimed. "Must be a'dozing in my crib. This real, Jack?"

"Reckon so," he said. "Figure it's what's got our boy here all tore up."

The muddy man babbled soundlessly on the trail, and dug his fingers into the hardpack earth.

Jack dropped his pack and untied the plastic jug from a side pocket. He shook it viciously– exoskeletons thumping around inside– and knelt beside the stranger. "Hold him," he said.

A bowmen dropped to his knees and wrenched the man's head to the side. He shoved his fingers into his upturned ear and dug out the muck within. "All clear, Daddy."

Jack uncorked the jug and dabbed out a dollop of dead insects. He tossed these into the brush and shook it again until a fat, wriggling earwig scampered across his palm. "In you go," he said, and pushed the bug– pincers first– into the prone man's ear.

The silent drivel he mouthed gained volume as the earwig's hindquarters disappeared into the cavity.

The bolt bowmen relinquished his hold and stepped back.

"Where'd you get the meth," Jack said and slapped the man across the face. Red slime blitzed out, and splashed his neck and lips. Jack tongued it, felt a minute zap spring through his nerves– tasted salt and copper. "By God," he said and licked his ruddy hand. "He's covered in the shit."

"Bah-bah-bah–" The man whimpered. "Ouchie! Bah-bah-bah! Bud! Buddy, Bud, Bud Temper."

"Bud Temper-what, boy? Where is he–?"

"Point us to the lair," Thin Ruby chimed in. "Where does this ol' Meth King shit his britches? In what direction will we suffer his foulness? Use your hole fiddlers if'n you ain't got the words. Show us, dagnabbit, or it's more'n just bugs in skulls for you."

"King is gone," the man proclaimed and sat up, straight as a plank. "Yaba-daba Doo, Buddy Temper's gone, and so are you," he sang.

"Que mierda?"

45

"Buddy Temper Doo, he sure is gone, baby, gone gone gone. Slut Knights had their way, had their say–"

"He's fried out," Jack said to the bowman. "Douse his ass for Daddy."

The bolt bow creaked as the platinum draw was pulled back. Thin Ruby yanked the weapon from his arms, spun it like a boomerang into the trailside scrub. "Hold it," he said. "What was that about Sluts? Speak, you sorry sap. Speak good or swallow bolts, by golly–"

"Slut Knights come and had theyselves a dandy old time. A real whopper, tell you what. Took it all. Took all they could and burned'er down. Right on down to the ground. Ground'a'Dabba Doo, and so are you!"

The Bald Knob cultists cackled in tandem. They slapped their knees with clicking claws. "Yabba-dabba," one of them cried. "Doo," the other moaned. Cloaks flapping, the cultists lay down on either side of the man– latched on to him like billowing leeches.

Thin Ruby turned away as they ate him raw.

XIV.

WHERE ONCE GREW BLACKBERRIES

THE CHAINDEVILS MARCHED THROUGH EUREKA IN silence and smoke. There were no birds, rodents, or cowering bodies to welcome them, and a sour odor cloistered the damp sky with furious intent. They passed blunts of cannabis and mugwort to still their anxious heads– huffed jars of excrement, sipped blackberry kratom slog– in an attempt to shake the bad meth.

The Bald Knob cultists hop-skipped to and fro through the haze, whispered secrets against each other's horns, and giggled like playmates.

Jack watched them from the corners of his eyes– prayed they would wander off into the burning smog and be gone. He assumed Earl's disappearance the night before had been their doing, and feared what twisted sights they had set on the day's bloody endeavors.

El Cazador drifted past with a lip full of hash. He led their sludge covered prisoner on a thin wire wound about his throat. Out of excitement or fear, he kicked at the man's naked cheeks with his leaden toe from time to time.

Just before sun up, they came upon a thicket that had choked the trail from passage. Chainsaws whined and cleavers fell. The smoke was so thick they could hardly tell flesh from branches. Sensing an outburst, a violent, flaring rash, Thin Ruby took up a song as they hacked at the wall of thorns:

"Come all hard men
And take given advice
Don't be in no hurry for t'die.
You'll think your'in dutch,
'Til your life is over
An' then you'll want asses for t'ride."
The others joined him:
"Well boys, keep away
from th' Reaper I say,
And give the ol' gal plenty of room.
For when you are dead,
No more suckin nor head
On th bald-headed end of your broom."

Hands gashed, and trail cleared, Jack and six Chaindevils pushed forward to scout the path ahead. They field dressed their smokes and slipped off their boots; padded softly at a swift pace with bows and chainsaws drawn. Within a hundred paces, the woods dropped off in a drastic slide of death and shale. The Chaindevils hunkered beside trunks of trees– watched Jack slither to the ledge– and waited.

As was foretold by the meth-lathered fool who had led them there, Jack discovered that Bud Temper and his compound had indeed been reduced to ashes. From where he stood– a dastardly rise that looked out over the destruction– he could see a handful of men milling about. Whether they were survivors, raiders, or bone picking vultures, Jack was not certain. He surmised the corpse spitroasted up the rectum on a tall, burning flagpole was most likely Bud Temper, and that the smoldering heap of rubble had once been the fabled amphetamine bordello. Fires raged across the valley in neon pinks and racer-snake greens; enormous tracks wound in and out through the mud: A caravan of war wagons.

One thing was for certain, the Slut Knights had up and gone with anything worth claiming.

Her Majesty's mission, the drugs, their salvation... everything was lost. No hope of ever getting it back. It was all over, and Jack knew it.

Prancer, a vicious saw-wielder with more hides to his name than even Jack, turned to him and asked what they ought do.

"Nothing," Jack replied. "Ain't no reason to pick through fresh Hell. We ain't gonna find nothing down there."

Prancer pushed his tears away.

"We'll dine on squirrel," Jack said, "and head for North come morning."

"I don't wanna go back," Prancer said and sat on the grass. "We got to find that meth. She'll have us skinned alive if we come back empty. Or worse yet, keep us out there in that fuckin' corn til I'm old as Ruby. Can't take another winter out there. I won't. We got to find them Sluts and–"

"And what, asshole? The fuck you mean?" Jack hauled Prancer up by his cowl of scalps and shook him. "Ain't nobody goes fussing with the Slut Knights lest you got a hankering to lose your cock. That what you want? A two foot buck-dirk down your pisser? You got the girth for that, big boy? Or do you wanna take air? And keep Thin Ruby out your goddamn mouth, you Baron-bottoming son'of'a'snake. Hope to God you live to be half the man he is."

"Oh, lay off him," a bolt bowmen said. He kicked out at nothing, and haughtily stalked up to Jack. "Ain't you got enough deductions? Let him be."

"You seen any of Her Majesty's vultures? Who's to say what killed who? Unless we got ourselves a snitch–"

The bowman racked a heavy rebar arrow from his sling. "Through with your shit," he said, and drew the platinum string.

Jack spun around as the bolt was loosed, and it skimmed across the side of his face. Everything turned to purples and sparks. Fuzzy bursts of light and sound. Throttle and vibrations. Warmth.

When he came to, Jack had his chainsaw buried in the bolt bowman's back. He yanked the gnashing band from side to side, widening the glorious chasm. Spine and skin chugged up and out– showered him with splinters. He was open-mouthed, and flexed his throat in a dry scream.

Prancer and the others stood back from the spray. They talked among themselves until Jack was through. After he had kicked the bowman's body off the edge of the cliff, he rejoined the group– head lowered in his shame.

The six of them walked back to the trail, and Jack could not bear to deliver the bad news to the others.

Thin Ruby could read it well enough on his blood-stained face. "It's over, y'all," the old man announced. "Time to go home."

"Ah-ah-ah," a Bald Knob cultist appeared beside him, waggled its claw in front of his nose.

"South," the other crooned from where it hid in the branches of a tree.

"We go South," they cackled.

El Cazador waited for the line to march on before he departed from their company. He stomped his leashed pet into the trees, made for the desolation beyond. The pair of them disappeared down the side of the cliff and into smoke and fire. "Andele," he said. "Surge forth or die."

XV.

ASSAULT ON THE LION'S DEN

THOUSANDS OF MOONS AGO– AFTER THE EARTH HAD burned to cinders– queer religious factions were the first new flowers to spring: Adolescent Gods rose in the tread of machines that had leveled the towns and cities of man, while older deities were reassembled by the strobing light of lead-belchers– Frankenstein'd together from their antiquated ruins– and retrofitted for the ages of horror that followed. Before political allegiances or territorial pissings bore the major fruits of future skirmishes, spiritual wars were carried out en masse. Abstract, regional cults identified themselves as clear victors in that decade of holy belligerence. Ancient Gods returned to their holes and one's faith became a matter of square acreage. Out with the old, in with shining waves of youthful zealotry.

Mother Time favors the bold, it would seem.

The Church of Daniel was one of few of these older religious orders to have survived the onslaught. Exiled worshippers of the bastard Nazarene, they kept their number small. The Daniels had amassed an obscene armory, and used their flame-cannons and napalm slings to breach the walls of the triumphant, heretical cults within their general vicinity. Try as the new Gods might to uproot the blood-frenzied monks, the order had resisted and remained.

Their Church– a circular dugout dubbed The Lion's Den– lay just a few miles South from where Bud Temper's ransacked compound smoked like a coal-cooked tater.

Knowing his history– of the Daniels having been long the ire of the Bald Knobbers– Thin Ruby alone understood where the cultists had led them. He looked out from the trees upon the squat bunker and shivered. *More bad business*, he thought; knew it was only a matter of time before they would reveal more drugs– dose up the Chaindevils– and set them to work.

As the old man expected, one of the foul, hulking Bald Knobbers hoisted Jack Pace by his loincloth, inverted him like Vitus on the cross, and shook out the hunk of Bud Temper's crystal onto the ground. The other cultist scooped up the red shard and crushed it between its clawed gauntlet; let the powder sift into their leather satchel of cursed blow.

"Here we go," Thin Ruby said to himself. "Out the pot and into the stove."

The Bald Knob cultists shepherded the Chaindevils into two groups. They doled out the mixture of meth, opiates, uppers, sluggers– God knows what– in thin lines on the tips of their knuckles. The men, each and every one of them, sniffed and snorted their allotment. Some collapsed, others wailed, and more still dropped to their knees to pleasure them-selves with the wet soil of two-weeks rain.

Jack's rage at having been upturned like a child was voided before the powders had even cleared his throat. Bliss overtook him. Splotches of thick paint skittered at the edges of his vision.

The Bald Knob cultist paused, held Jack with tenderness, and whispered in his ear.

Jack listened. The words filling him with hard, quasi

sexual longing for destruction. Darkness and hate filled his every pore.

With a snicker and a skip, the cultist moved on to the next man– gave him his toot and marching orders likewise.

The violence would be *good*, Jack promised himself. He could be pure this time: Pain-bringer of Her Majesty's will, he would slash limbs, carve faces into new shapes, and leave them breathing. "Well," he said aloud, "few of 'em at least. Daddy can do that. I can leave a few. Yessir, yes I can. You just watch." He babbled on and on.

The chansawman beside him– deaf to the conversation– humped into a tree notch until his member was chaffed and bleeding.

Thin Ruby took his dose slowly, waited for the Bald Knobber to move along, and casually hocked out as much as he could with a careful, quiet sneeze. Whatever amount of the narcotic he did not expel hit him across the brain within moments. *Easy now*, he thought and stayed on his feet.

"Look'y here, y'all," Jack addressed the moaning ranks of Chaindevils. "The enemy lies yonder," he pointed out the bunker, hopped in place, and ground his sparse, black teeth. "Christ lovers, pederasts, and father-fuckin' holy-rollers, all of them. We might've failed our mission, but fear not, boys! Our brother Bald Knobbers done offered us another way out: Waste the freaks– enemies of Her Majesty– and our days in the corn are over. So grab them saws, hang those bolts, and let's roar these blood-drinkin' bigots right on back to Bethlehem."

Whoops and meth-addled ramblings ensued.

"Hush up, now," Thin Ruby hissed. "These ain't unarmed merchants. We got to go in quiet like. Dancer's toes and the grace of cats. Slink or be still. Them wretches ain't gonna take it lying down so we best–"

A sharp click came from behind the old man. The boombox rattled to life, spewed blast-beats and galloping electric strings. Music embraced the wind and was carried far out across the hills.

Thin Ruby turned, slack-jawed with fury, and glared at the Bald Knobbers.

The cultist held the stereo out in front of it, stuck out a fat, purple tongue. Waggled it back and forth. It's twin banged it's masked head in time with with the drums, and sent its tasseled horns flailing. "Slaughter," they croaked together.

"Slaughter," Jack Pace cried.

Thin Ruby shook his head as the others mimicked the call: A thunderous gasp which sailed above the boombox, drowned its bass in their timber and tone. The first starter-line was ripped– Jack's, of course– and he followed, sullen and helpless, as the Chaindevil horde advanced on the Lion's Den.

They were within a hundred feet of the stone bunker when the Daniels emerged from within. Armed with billow-torches and egg shaped swords, they clambered sluggishly from the square flaps of steel set in stone. Clad in their white, cast-iron armor, they moved with a slow grace.

"Lo," the Daniels chanted, pushing deep from within the recesses of their throats. The thick, bullet helmets amplified their voices: A zenith of airy vibration– lungs as hallowed Cathedrals.

Jack threw back his head, and belted an old verse in reply– one they had learned from Thin Ruby:

"It's adieu to ol' Jesus,
Farewell to God-Christ,
I'll chainsaw your Father
For Her Majesty's spite."
The Chaindevils raised their saws, aimed their bolts, gripped their cleavers, and sang:
"Well, I wish you all to maggots,
And myself to better grace.
So lay out your necks,

And I'll not aim for your face."

As the Chaindevils neared, the brutish monks doused their blades with spritzes of oil from their billowers, and set them ablaze with a quick pump.

"Behold," the Daniels cried: A chorus of iron-rimmed voices.

The bowmen skidded to a halt and loosed their bolts– showered the Daniels in barbed rebar and makeshift skewers. Some of their projectiles glanced off the sturdy white shields with a pong. Others found their mark, embedding iron shrapnel and hooks into sternums and fragile arteries.

Those who wielded the storied chainsaws ducked low or swung high; swirled their coughing bands of teeth against knee braces, or into the thin break between cowl and shoulder pad. Cleavers tethered to their wrists by thick man-leathers, Thin Ruby and the meat hackers chopped and slashed at the stumbling wounded. The old man yanked his blade free from the groin of his prey, noticed the boombox had ceased its profane beat. He turned back to the tree-line: The Bald Knob cultists were nowhere to be seen.

Well armored and undeterred, few of the Daniels fell upon the first, crucial wave of assault, and instead blitzed their flaming swords in all directions– shot gouts of ivory flame at anyone who dared approach the Lion's Den.

Six of the Chaindevil bowmen were swallowed by their fire; skin and meat dripped and pooled about their bare femurs. Bone charred and crackled, sifted into drifting ashes taken by the wind. Small black puddles on the field grass marked their passage from life into death, and nothing more.

Prancer dodged a blast from a billower as he parried his saw against the monk's blade. He pledged a hardy stance, lashed out at the flame-thrower, and gored it in a flash of spark and fumes.

The Daniel glanced at his ruined weapon and took

another slash to the helmet. Black stars twirled in his eyes. He fumbled his hilt, dropped the sword, and re-leveled the oil gurgling billower at Prancer's face. The Daniel clicked his igniter.

Prancer was blown free of his boots as the Daniel's weapon imploded. The Chaindevil dropped his saw in mid-air, and it landed on a comrade– a cleaver wielder called Carl– with a wet thwack. Prancer sailed through the encroaching darkness like a fish-tailed meteor– cratered against a tall oak in a burst of blood and organs. Carl perished shortly thereafter as he reeled from the head wound, and his combatant staved in his chest with a fiery sword.

The blast had hurled back and breached the walls of the bunker. A glorious crack in the stone which smoked and crumbled; welcomed the assailants with its gaping glimmer. Disarmed Daniels scurried within, and put out fires with their tactical hoses and brass snuffers. The flames spread, and those who were not armored caught fire in their white robes of gauze.

Jack Pace was the first infidel through the hole– into the Lion's Den. He was followed promptly by seven screaming chainsaws, and seven angry men.

"Come get it," Jack said. "Let's have those necks."

XVI.
REVELRY

THREE DAYS AFTER THE BATTLE AT THE LION'S DEN, the victorious Chaindevils made camp in the center of a township named Briarwood Estates. The community consisted of several ancient structures: Rare, wooden lodgings that once housed prehistoric men and which were well maintained having survived the near unanimous devastation of world-ending war. The buildings had been converted through the ages into churches, kingdoms, brothels– was once a museum curated by a particularly mad and wealthy Branson Baron just prior to his demise.

Now, the Briarwood structures served as a series of watering-holes and drug-dens: A haven for battle hounds to lick their wounds, celebrate lives so easily lost, and spend their spoils. Protected and owned by the Bootheel Mutant Collective– those twisted, savage pilgrims from the Southeast wastelands– the Estates operated under a system of truce. Quarrels were to be settled as individuals, passer-by were not to be disturbed. Murderous whims were to be paid in full, random acts of violence were not tolerated. Failure to comply with these terms resulted in swift decapitation by the garoutte of a shark-eyed mutant, or worse yet, a fallout injection of tainted groundwater. A fate which either granted a slow, agonizing death or assimilation and bodily evolution into the Bootheel Collective.

Here, they celebrated victory, buried their dead, and waited for the Bald Knob cultists to return. Without their masked escorts, concern had grown among: Were they allowed back in Her Majesty's land? Had they achieved what She sought?

Each man silently prayed that the decimation of the Daniels was enough to warrant release from the Field of Pain. In growing panic– as autumnal winds whispered the promise of winter– the Chaindevils numbed their fear with all manner of self-destructive deeds.

Though the Estates had weathered humans and monsters of all loping gaits, Her Majesty's Chaindevils were, perhaps, more than even the mutants could control.

"Bring out the needles," Thin Ruby said. He gestured wildly at the legless barkeep and shouted. "We need torches and spoons, by God."

The barkeep gripped the counter, pushed its seat down the aluminum track that ran the length of the bar, and rolled to another, quieter patron.

"Cain't you hear? Or did the father'fuckin woolybugger what took your knees put a stopper in them ears while they was at it? I been all the way to Hell for to bash baby Jesus in his manger, and here you is not paying me no mind. Why, I ought to–"

"Calm it down," a Bootheel bouncer put its ten-fingered hand on the old man's shoulder. "Don't talk to him that'a'way."

Jack Pace dropped the brass pipe he had been sucking– let it clatter on his small table near the window. The stocky hacker seated across from him rose in his seat. "Hands off," Jack said.

"Tell your ol' Paw to watch his mouth," the mutant began, "and we won't have no–"

Jack's stool turned on its side as he leapt to his feet. "I said," Jack and the hacker moved to the bar, "take your sick-dick greasers off of him."

Thin Ruby, still in the bouncer's clutch, continued to holler obscenities at the barkeep. He spoke and acted as if danger was not grasping the soft pool of his neck. "The needle, damn you! Bring out the fire and I'll not take ye for my supper. Grind you down to them nubs and boil your–"

"Back off," the mutant turned on Jack and the hacker. Lime ooze wriggled in the corners of its torn lips. A bionic eye purred and clicked, centered on the Chaindevils, widened. "I mean it," the mutant said.

Jack and the hacker broke off– took alternating paths to the counter– each to one side of the Bootheel bouncer. They kept a steady pace, and stared it down as they stalked.

"It don't got to be like this," the mutant said. It relinquished it's hold on Thin Ruby– reached for the drill-shooter. "Stop right there."

The old man having been turned loose, Jack Pace and the hacker stopped in their tracks; pursued the conflict no further.

"I'd take twenty ruddy mule-boys over one sorry fuck as you," Thin Ruby tossed an empty tumbler at the barkeep. The glass plopped in its lap, tapped both testicles, and sent it gagging with pain. "Gimme my spoon!"

The Bootheel mutant snaked it's rusted arm out and grabbed Thin Ruby around the throat. It lifted the Chaindevil out of his seat– held him off the ground– and watched him turn violet. "Why you–"

Jack Pace lunged at the bouncer. With one leg extended, he stomped the mutant's knee back into the bar. An excruciating snap rang out.

The hacker shimmied a filet knife from a holster sewn into the flesh of his naked thigh. He dropped low in a flash of silver, waved the blade at the mutant's groin, and stepped back.

The thin fur pants worn by the bouncer fell around it's ankles. The mutant gripped his exposed, necrotic manhood as dauber yellow blood and black semen spewed from the it's crotch between decagon hands.

Thin Ruby, released once more, fell to the floor on his buttocks. "Die," he hollered. "Die, you foul suckler of ruined earth!"

Jack hauled him up by the armpits.

The mutant-gutting hacker held out his knife– clotted with dark– and glared at the onlookers.

"Feast upon the brine of cold death," Thin Ruby said. He kicked at the sputtering corpse and spat in it's milky eye as he was hauled out the door. "Want my spoon, dagnabbit."

The hacker sheathed the blade down his leg. "Figure we got about fifteen minutes," he said and turned to Jack. "We gonna stand?"

"Ain't another option comes to mind."

"Uh-huh." He burrowed his eyes into Jack's as they plodded away from the saloon. "It's just–"

Jack curled his eyebrow into a sickle moon.

" –the jailer's gonna want him." The hacker nodded at the strung out old man between them; kept his eyes tethered to Jack's.

"I'm gonna pretend I ain't registered what it is you're suggesting, Lilac." Jack stepped in front of Thin Ruby and bent forward.

Lilac boosted him up by the seat of his loincloth, onto Jack's back.

"You just play round-up–" Jack hoisted the old man upright, grabbed his limp arms " –and get ready for the shit."

"Right on," Lilac shrugged and jogged ahead. He whistled three quick beats: A signal to gather the others from their various slumbers and slumps throughout the Estate. "Soo-wee," he cried.

Jack carried Thin Ruby to the Chaindevil camp– ignored his vocal rampages and weak attempts to be set free. Once the pair had sat beside their fire, Marsha emerged naked from one of their tents. "Hidy," he said.

Through the flaps, a thick legged mutant whore held a needle to its arm, and moaned for the cleaver wielder to return.

"You stable?" Jack asked.

"Sure," Marsha replied. He regarded Thin Ruby's sorry state and asked: "What'd he do?"

"Take a guess."

"Gonna have at least fifty on us. They packing slugs? Seen one with a bandolero when we first come through."

"Reckon they'll be breaking out whatever they got right about now–"

A bolt rifle sounded off. Three quick whumps– close enough that the tinkling of shells could be heard from camp. A mutant yakked and screamed.

Jack Pace clicked his teeth, slapped Thin Ruby across the face. "God damn you," he said.

"God damn us all," Thin Ruby replied. "We are the shit-house dogs: Paid nothing for everything. We was made to circle the pit of human waste. We wasn't born'd, we was made, I say again." His blueish lips frothed– trembled with rage. "We ain't right. We take and take. We got no Gods, no masters. We ain't bowed to no one 'cus we ain't got the brains to serve. We just subsist on the tit we was given. We don't push our fangs to no nipple, but only on account of what happens to bad dogs who bite the wrong breast. We ain't here for no Bald Knobbers. We ain't here for *Her Majesty*," Thin Ruby grabbed Jack by the ears, pulled him closer to his fury, "We cain't suckle forever, Jack. Them Bald Knobbers ain't through with us. They'll be back. Cain't you see it? See me, boy. Hear me. Let this old bitch spell it all out for ye. Please, Jack. Oh, please."

61

Jack pushed him away, rubbed his face, and listened.

"We was boys once– all of us –babies, even. Boys brought to the corn for the sins of the earth. Dropped naked, full of meanness and sorrow; given to the predators for to cull or to raise. And raised you were, or killed were your unburdened brothers– dashed of brain or stripped of humanity. Only two choices beneath her Majesty's iron claw, see? But I was more than a boy. I have lived, Jack. I've run the banks of rivers with my head held high. I've known the warmth of a heart that beats beyond the pressure of a swollen cock. I've had a mother and a father and brothers who were blood and a sister who was cherished and I watched them all fucking die in the pit I now circle and I see their faces down there– swollen and sad, nothing to say, only the memories of those spare moments when pain and Hell and death come a'ripping– and you cain't ever know what horrors lie in them faces. All you can do is add and add as we take and take until all that's left is us. We'll howl– yessir, we will– but ain't no one gonna answer."

"Thought I ain't had hopes or dreams no more. Thought they went to the shitter like everything else what give me cause to call myself a man. And then you come along. A cub with brains as long as your fangs. A dog with a soul. I seen it in your eyes, Jack. And seeing your'n liked to have raised mine from the grave. You brought me back. You give me the strength to question, to *see*. And all I ever wanted was for you to see it too. The pit don't have to be all we know. There are mountains and caves– rivers that ain't all gone to turds– better titties, greener wastelands. I want you to find it, by God. I want you to hold your arms out and breathe."

Jack stared at the fire. "I don't know what–"

The sound of racing feet cut him short.

"Hope them are ours," Marsha said. "Hold on–" the hacker rose and returned to his tent.

The mutant sat up and jerked forward with stars in its eyes. "Lay down," it said.

The tent shuttered close. Wet smacks and a flurry of whimpers came from within. A hollow clang, followed by silence.

Jack looked away, and made to whisper his thoughts to Thin Ruby– would tell him everything he needed to say. But the old man's tongue stuck out from one corner of his lips, and his nose whined with dust and misuse. Passed out from the festivities of his latest slaughter in a lifetime of destruction– the victory they shared as hounds of the shit-house.

Jack realized everything he had ever done– everything he could recall of his life– he had done beside the ancient killer dozing before the flames. Sleeping so like the baby he had once been.

Marsha pushed through the flaps– all black stains, a tricking lake of ebon– and dragged his cleaver behind him.

Jack shook himself loose of whatever spell had been cast. "Sorry for your loss," he said, and grinned. "Hope it ain't cost you much."

Marsha shrugged, wiped the enormous blade on a charred log. "So she goes," he said.

XVII.
HOUNDS O' WAR

JACK PACE PUSHED HIS JAGGED FINGERNAILS INTO the wound and found a smooth mass within. Hot to the touch, he pulled at the slug with what little energy he had left. It came free with a sloshing sound and a spurt of blood leapt from his sternum. Fueled by one last fireside toot of the late Bud Temper's red meth, the Chaindevil had hardly felt the impact at all, even as a purple-black bruise spread across his chest.

Night had fallen, but the storm of Bootheel mutant bolt rifles lit the sky like God's own fury. War was waged by strobes of lead laden white and bursts of fiery ember. Guttural gunshot formed the chorus of battle– the screams of man and mutant like a rattling tin-can beat. Chainsaws gnashed as cleavers fell in the streets, and platinum bowstrings twanged from the roof of every saloon.

In an attempt to slow a seemingly endless stream of armed Bootheel mutants, the Chaindevils employed every fearsome tactic in the dark book of their creed: They carved off the Collective's abnormal faces to don them as masks; took hostage their barkeeps, merchants, and sex-workers– destroyed their children with their bare heels and teeth in the gutters; ate the necrotic flesh from living torsos, resulting in torrents of vomit and sickness...

None of which stopped the assault.

Jack Pace– bleeding, laughing– knew that they would not survive the night. This would be their final stand. Come sunlight, the Chaindevils would be no more. He turned his streaming eyes to his feet where Thin Ruby still slept. Pieces of hacked mutant lay in heaps all around the old man like a putrid, protective circle of twitching meat. The corpse that had shot Jack in the chest issued yellow blood from its throat– showered them with grime from where it lay.

At the corner of their camp, he watched Marsha deflect a slug with his great cleaver; three more shots removed his kneecaps and the hacker fell. A Bootheel mutant approached from behind, leveled a pump-action burst gun, and blew Marsha's head open. Another pump– the Chaindevil's neck erupted in smoke and bone– and he was gone from this world forever more. Without even his last fuck to remember him; held only in memory by Jack Pace and his sixty-some-odd comrades who remained.

It was perhaps the death of Marsha– or the dozing destroyer at his feet– which pushed Jack's brain to the extremities of resolve. For despite what lengths he had gone to make an animal of himself– the innocents he had slain, Field Pirates he had ingested, mule-boys he had abused, the degenerates he had loved– despite a loathing for civility at large, Jack Pace was still a human all told. He dropped his saw, let his bearded chin tip down to his blackened chest, and sagged.

Jack made a bench of a severed torso, sat down, and retrieved the bundle of grass from his satchel. With his last, tattered, tobacco skin, the Chaindevil rolled himself a blunt. He lit it with a coal pricked from their fire. His ears felt full of cotton. Too quiet.

Jack stroked Thin Ruby's knotted mane, took a puff, and sang.

"Goodbye to all,
Farewell to ol' Paw.
Don't wait on me to arrive.
I've gone away,
Won't see no more days.
But at least I've got smoke in my eyes."

The old man stirred in his sleep. His lips fluttered, and he let out a long, low croak. Jack thought he was going to be sick, and began to turn him on his side. Thin Ruby pushed his hands away, and sang:

"S'long, dear Maw,
I'm sorry I've gone.
Don't count on me to survive."

The Bootheel Mutant Collective advanced towards camp to the old man's ragged tune.

The Chaindevils– now down to their last thirty heads– had fallen back to the fire. They regrouped with the two men who were, perhaps, the deadliest, most storied champions among them, and felt a tingle of comfort in their presence.

Together, the Chaindevils cried out:

"This world's a killer,
And I ain't no quitter.
But God don't like it when I'm high."

Partially shielded by Jack's wall of bodies, they docked their last bolts, gassed up their saws, and readied their knives. The mutant forces circled them. They laughed with mirthless pleasure; jeered in victory at their cornered quarry.

"Yes, this world's a killer," Jack brayed– a high, broken yodel.

Thin Ruby rose on rubber legs. "And I am a sinner," he chanted.

The Chaindevils clawed their chests, stamped their feet. Every living mouth screamed: "But you sorry cunts ain't taking us alive!"

Upon refrain of their furious chorus, as if in answer, a howl echoed through the streets: A monstrous call of brutality– the most beastial of desolate cries. The inhuman keening chilled the fluids racing through the veins of all who heard it. Mutants paused their approach, and the Chaindevils held tight to their weapons. They searched about, and peered into darkness choked by bolt-fog.

Another howl rumbled into pricked ears.

Lilac leaned into Jack Pace and asked: "The fuck is that?" The hacker had traded his cleaver for the bloody chainsaw of a fallen comrade. Unaccustomed to its weight, he held it like a cane, and took deep, sucking breaths of panic.

Jack did not reply. His eyes had centered on a black shape in the distance. Blacker than the night, thick as smoke, it grew larger. A pair of green gems– beacons in the void– drew closer to the circle of fire and death.

"Andale," a familiar voice hollered.

The howl erupted all around them– cloaked the crackle of flames and murmurs of men.

"Hell fire," Jack said.

A gargantuan figure burst through the Bootheel ranks. Mutants bubbled up through the air like loosed vultures at a tentside Bald Knob sermon. They flew against arcs of their own gore, padded against their airborne brothers, and cascaded back down to earth. The great, galloping shadow picked them up in fours and fives– flung them again and again.

As the mutants scattered and broke ranks before the rampaging giant, Jack Pace saw it: A black dog of unbelievable size. A God of fur and fang. Taller than a Field Schooner, wide as a boulder. Snarling and insane. Blood-tinged plumes of rancid breath floated from its dripping jaws. It's smile was painted in red and it panted for violence.

Astride the hound of war, El Cazador laughed with a frenzy to match his mount. "Muerte," he commanded, and spun his illustrious, hungry rifle on the mutants.

Their screams and death-rattles were drowned out by the low, droning growl of the beast. They were consumed whole, or shaken until their tongues wagged free from the root. Their elongated heads erupted in beats of three.

Click-clack, cried the reload.

Pop-pop-pop-

The mutants turned to flee– bolt rifles cracked and pump shottys blared in their desperate retreat.

The mutants began to depart, but the Chaindevils regained their aim, shrugged their shrouds of starry wonder.

The mutants ran, and chainsaws followed.

XVIII.
EL CAZADOR

TWO DAYS SOUTH OF HER MAJESTY'S BORDER, THE Chaindevils marched for home. They had stripped the Estates of its remaining narcotics, weapons, and groceries– stuffed their packs and burned what they could not carry in a bon. Bundles of low-grade meth and slug canisters were strapped to the great, black dog. Four scrawny Field Pirate outposts– pillaged along the route– had provided more clean meat than could ever be consumed. Even the belly of El Cazador's ravenous mount swayed with the fullness of many raw men.

Thin Ruby and the hackers trailed the rifleman atop his hound. They breathed deep the rank musk in its loping tread; found religion in the shadow of their fanged savior. The few surviving bowmen– now armed with salvaged bolt guns– limped along with meanness set in their teeth.

Jack Pace and the sawmen held the front of the line. Lilac had taken to the chainsaw, carried it with pride. Though their loads were heavy, and mourning ripened in their hearts, the men held their heads high, sang new songs of glory.

As they marched, the Chaindevils asked the rifleman how he had come upon the black dog. Beneath a sky the color of crisp, autumn apples, El Cazador told them his story;

explained that he had taken his leave in Eureka after deciding a man such as Bud Temper would have more treasures to discover– that a caravan of Slut Knights would not be so diligent as to uncover all of the compound's secrets. And so he had taken the mule-boy to its ruins, hoping to reclaim some manner of physical accomplishments with which to buy their freedom.

Thin Ruby could make no sense of his words, and so departed their company for to defecate among the trees.

El Cazador shrugged, and continued: He told them the Slut Knights had indeed destroyed or made off with everything of value– a miraculous, and terrifying feat. It chilled him to see the scope of their strength; the power of feminine might by way of ten thousand grimacing dead left in their wake– another thousand in the process of joining the lost.

Amid the horrors– the sharp edged void of human extremes– El Cazador had found the pit: A hole of stone, a cavern of bones. And inside the pit, the great hound had emerged with a thirst for vengeance on its lolling purple tongue. The rifleman said that he spoke with the beast. He told it the stories of his life– sang the sweetest and bawdiest ballads he knew. That night, they dined together on the mule-boy, and by morning man and dog returned to the trail.

El Cazador began to regale them the stories of their journey through Arkansas when The Guy– a bolt bowmen, called so for his inauspicious brand of plainness– coughed and elbowed Jack. "I just hate to interrupt y'all," he said, nodded at El Cazador, "but them Bald Knobbers is yonder." He pointed North.

The rifleman and his audience about-faced on the trail. All nervous shuffles and bleached faces, they adjusted their gaze. Eyes were alighted by the appearance of the horned devils, not ten yards off from where they stood.

One of the cultists beckoned to them with a long finger. The other crouched on all fours, kicked up dust with its legs.

It began to bark and lunge at them, as if in mockery of the black dog whose hackles raised upon notice of the strange display.

The dog's eyes– roasted almonds, pitted with black– rolled in its head. Maddened by the cultist's appearances, or by their ability to slip past its innate senses, no man could say, but the dog snarled and snapped. The sound of its jaws was like a bolt-shot.

The Bald Knob cultist climbed onto the back of its brother. It gripped the other by the horns of its mask, and spurred its ribs. They galloped down the trail towards the Chaindevils– stopped just short of El Cazador and the hound.

"Arf-arf," mimed the crawling cultist.

The black dog howled in its face: A hot gust of snot and anger. Flecks of pinkish schmaltz spewed from its mouth and slicked the Bald Knobbers in their black robes.

When the tumult of throat-thunder had settled, the cultist resumed its barking: "Arf-arf arf-arf!"

El Cazador bucked upon the hump of its back as the great dog whined and shook. "Easy," he said, speaking softly to it. "Estate quieto."

"Give," the Bald Knob rider said. It held out its palm, snapped its knuckles. "Give it."

"Arf-arf!"

Jack looked about– confused. "Give what?"

"Esta bien," El Cazador whispered.

"The dog," the cultist said. From the billowing depths of its cloak, a knife was produced. The blade was fashioned in a Bowie design– as was custom in their Kingdom– but it had been warped, stretched, and twisted. A cruel, swerving razor that glinted red in the morning light. "God blood," the Bald Knobber said, and waved the knife along its shoulder like a fiddle bow.

The great dog took a step back, and its enormous paws

73

unearthed a vein of shale in the dirt. A high moan escaped its lips.

"Arf-"

El Cazador began to cry.

" –arf-arf-arf!"

Jack Pace opened his mouth as if to speak. His throat went slack, and his cheeks filled with sour spit. *Do it*, he thought. *Do it*.

Lilac reached across his chest, pulled him back.

"El es mi amigo," El Cazador said, teeth dripping with tears.

"Arf-arf-bitch!" The crawling cultist laughed at the rifleman.

"Down," the other demanded, "get down." It pointed at the trail with its knife. "Give it."

El Cazador braced the rifle against his shoulder. He ground his teeth, began to raise the stock. "No," he said.

From behind the horned abominations, Thin Ruby rose. A pale, leathered snake with eyes of snow. His cleaver ascended– high above the Bald Knob rider– and flashed like fire. "Get thee behind me, you cum-crusted welps!"

The Bald Knobber turned upon his crooked mount. It's black eyes flitted between the elderly hacker and the cleaver above. "Ope," it said.

Thin Ruby brought down his blade– a parallel swoop– and carved the cultist at the waist. Severed in two, it's torso slipped from its nethers and fell to the ground. The legs– still clinging to the sides of its brother– twitched and fidgeted. Blood poured from the separated hunks; spewed hot sticky red like an Oklahoma geyser.

"Die, scum!" Thin Ruby raised his cleaver once more–

–The crawling cultist hop-frogged to one side, bucked the dead legs from its back, and scooped up the twisted Bowie knife–

–The hacker's blade took root in bloody soil with a thud.

Jack Pace ripped himself free of Lilac's clutches. He yanked the chainsaw from the sling across his back. His legs pumped him forward.

The Bald Knobber leapt from the ground and jammed the knife into Thin Ruby's chest.

"Well," the old man said. Bile dribbled between his lips. He gasped as the cultist dragged the Bowie down the length of his sparse belly. Coils of stomach burst with a pop. Piss and excrement leapt between the blade and his ravaged insides.

Jack ripped the starter line. The saw sputtered to life and he arced it back behind his ears. It's teeth grazed a strand of his oily locks, chewed them up and spat them into the wind.

El Cazador called out to him, rifle raised. He could not obtain a clear sight, hollered again and again. The great black dog howled. Lilac and the sawmen scrambled. Bolt rifles clicked and leather straps creaked.

Jack heard nothing.

The Bald Knob cultist tugged the Bowie until it cascaded through Thin Ruby's groin. It shucked free of him with a choral twang.

The old man fell into his growing pool of gore. He briefly pushed his fists against the earth, and then was still. His last breath having been composed of filth and mud, Thin Ruby passed on and was no more.

Without word nor cry, the Chaindevil closed the distance between them. The cultist, still down on all fours, looked up at Jack and cocked its masked head to one side. For an instant, Jack saw the idiot behind the horns: A blabbering, black-toothed fool. Eyes without light. Brains like floating pondshit. A blunted tool of fear. So much like his own.

He whacked at the Bald Knobber's face, sliced it away from bone– mask and all. The featureless zealot clawed at the air. It seized up and began to belch blood from an exposed length of esophageal tubing. Jack kicked it in the chest, bent it over backwards with a sick crunch, and pounced. Against the torrent of hot fluids, the Chaindevil hacked at the cultist with his chainsaw, slammed its gnashing teeth against flesh. Human mass morphed into liquid and spongy rubble. Jack bashed and carved until nothing was left but a lake of ooze on the trail. Blood fumes and bonesmoke filled his withered lungs.

When he was through, Jack Pace turned back to his comrades, and found himself alone.

XIX.

JACK IN THE WOODS OR "THE WARLOCK AND THE BALD KNOBBERS"

Deep in the bosom of the Ozark hills, he walked and spoke to himself: Long nights, spiteful thoughts. Beside ichor streams, he slept and shivered: Dry of mouth, dead of gumption. Six days without drug or drink, he shat and vomited: Nightmares and pain consumed him.

He buried the chainsaw– his only lover– in a shallow grave of sand.

The Goddess of the woods came to him on the seventh morning of his exile. He sat upon a rock beside a low fire of moist leaves. With eyes that did not move, he stared out at the face of a cliff above the boney creek bed. The Goddess hobbled across the bank on twin ivory canes, her face obscured by long gray locks. Her robes billowed about her like a bustling badger, and she walked with confidence towards the killer on the stone.

Through his own palpable musk, Jack could smell her: Alien flowers, and crushed walnuts– an oily, vinegar scent. The flesh of the elderly.

Her humped back popped as she bent her face to his, and she opened her robe– gripped him by the hair with her leather fingers. The Goddess pushed his face into the folds of her stomach; held him so that he was forced to take air from her dusty skin.

"I claim you," she told him.

"Keep me," he replied, mouth mashed against her.

"Doubtful," she answered. "To the highest bidder you'll go."

He cried for a while and she stroked his head.

"Before I take you away," she said, "I can tell you a story of the Earth."

He nodded. His tears burned and itched.

"Listen close," she said, "and tell me what you see."

ELI RODE on through the hills until his mule could go no further. He dug in his heels but the mount wheezed and stomped. Its ribs trembled against his inner thighs and sent tremors down to the depths of his cheap horsehide boots. The mule parked itself beside a lone maple, head lowered, and snorted miserably.

Eli spat and got down from the saddle. He tipped his wide brimmed hat and glared at the sky: The sun was high, as it had been for longer than the natural order of things should allow. Too hot for the season and with nary a winter's cloud to shield him, his head throbbed. He wore no shirt beneath the canvas bibs and his skin was burnt and taught where exposed around the straps. The air felt broken. Disassembled.

This was his doing, he knew.

Undoing, he reconsidered. *The power of mine hand hath wrought for me a deposition of Earth and Heaven. But what becomes of Hell?*

As if in reply, a rifle shot cracked the air. The bullet breached a low hanging branch beside the mule. Splinters and pulp dusted Eli's naked shoulder. He hunkered low and pulled the shotgun from its saddle sling. From a slight rise, he spied dark figures scrambling through the trees.

Hell is here, he thought. *Unchanged and emboldened under the tutelage of my idiocy.*

"I seen him," a voice said, obscured within the shadows of the wood. "Got eyes on the mule."

Eli looked at the beast and panic spread across his chest. *Slay not the innocent,* he prayed, *spare me the loss of this child of God.*

The mule cast Eli a sidelong glance. Fear of the bullet lay heavy in its bloodshot gaze, yet it did not move. Either too beat, too stubborn, or perhaps unwilling to accept the haste at which men betray their sense of compassion and mercy.

Eli uncurled from a crouch. He laid down on the warm scrub, belly flat. Shotgun extended. *Enter mine threshold, receive thy pain.*

"Don't you aim for no mule," another voice replied.

A measure of ease allowed his racing heart to quiet, but Eli kept his finger crooked to the trigger.

"That sum'bitch kill't my horse. I ain't walkin' back to town."

He recalled the dead steed with abstract sorrow: The poor creature caught a four-finger spread of his buckshot six miles back. Eli had miscalculated the turn and so the horse went down as he cranked out a shell at its rider. He thought the man who spoke would surely have died screaming beneath his steed had the sky not been illuminated by an alien sun. Abandoned by his brethren, he imagined, had the blanket of night been allowed its usual reign.

The fault for this was his to carry. He and the dark magics he had employed to find the stump.

"Up here," the horseless rider said. Two black horns peered out from behind a tree.

For my sins, I suffer the judgment of Twin Fathers. One

Lord to damn me, Eli cocked the shotgun. *And one to celebrate that which I have damned.*

A masked face revealed itself. Black of hood, white of eyes and mouth. Red tassels spewed from the tips of both horns; bands of ivory wrapped thrice around their bases. Crude white stitches raked the Devil's chin like a wretched beard. Guise of a demon. Motif of these damnable souls who roamed the hillside and called themselves Bald Knobbers.

Eli held his breath.

"I seen his hat," the Bald Knobber said. He held a rifle clubwise; his last bullet having been spent in the boughs beside the mule, or else some miles back in the history of this now lengthy pursuit.

One Father above. Eli inched the dovetail sight across the dirt. He squinted until his aim came to rest below the horns. *One Father below.*

The Bald Knobber turned to the left and laid eyes on the barrel pointed at his head. "Well, shit," he said.

Eli pulled the trigger.

The mask exploded in a flurry of bone and blood. Gunsmoke filled Eli's nostrils. He watched the headless vigilante take three steps forward before his legs crumpled like paper. The mule began to bray and kick wildly in place, its energies apparently restored. Eli cocked back the second round and waited.

"By God." Someone shouted, further down the slope. "This ol' boy done kill't Pruitt."

"You sure?"

Eli shuddered at the gruff voice.

"I'm sure as shit, Bull. The man's head come clear off his neck."

"Well, Hell," Bull Walker said.

"Hell's right," the Baldknobber answered. "Your goddamned *warlock* brought it right'chere. Devil's domain, fire of the sun, and all. We ain't never gonna be clean of this."

"Shutter those flappin' lips," Bull replied "Don't wanna' hear no nonsense. I want that bastard dead."

"May not want to hear it," the Baldknobber said, "but you the one what hired him in the first place. Now we got to fix what he done, God help us all."

"If you ain't hard enough to march up that there hill," Bull said, "I'll do it my damn self."

Eli sucked in another breath. *Be it the Lord God or Satan Himself*, he raised the sight to meet the crest of the hill, *let me vanquish this King of Grubs in thy hallowed names.*

From the day he was hired by the Baldknobbers, Eli found that Bull Creek Walker, their founder and leader, was a man who often got what he was after.

Tall, brutal, and compelled by righteous ignorance, the vigilante general had accomplished his mission of bush-whacking terrorism with little effort. The corpses of Judge Calhoun's twin boys, found gutted in a sycamore, had struck fear into the heart of every farmer and corrupt official in the county. Men were brutalized. Wives and daughters were whipped in the streets. Unchecked and spurious spawn of wealthy county chairmen were spared their comeuppances no longer. The hills had belonged to Bull and his Baldknobbers thereafter.

Though also of notoriety among locals, Eli, too, was afraid.

The servant of Gods should not shiver by the light of another man, he thought. *And yet...*

A twig snapped behind him.

Duped by the duplicitous.

"Hold it, warlock." Bull spat. "Move and I'll send your ass to Jesus. Or Hell. Whichever foolish kingdom'll take ye."

Eli let loose his hold on the stock. His trigger finger unclenched and he let the shotgun down onto the soil. He turned, ever so slightly, to see the Baldknobber chief standing across his legs. A rifle was pointed at his back.

"You're gonna undo whatever it is you done," Bull said. He nodded at the wayward sun. "Put that damn moon back where it belongs and take us to the stump."

Before Eli could reply, the mule reared back and jumped. The hooves of the beast whipped out to one side and took Bull off his feet. The Baldknobber's chest crunched noisily and he spun off down the slope.

"Hellfire," a voice came from below the rise. "He's plugged Bull!"

"He ain't shot," another replied. "You hear a shot go off? Pull the cotton out your ears."

Bull moaned from somewhere in the brush.

Eli hauled up the shotgun and stood. He took hold of the saddle horn, tried to calm the mule. It brayed and kicked wildly as if held by a fever of the brain. He spoke sweet to the beast and rubbed its sweaty neck, but the mule would have none of it.

May mine burro laugh at fear and be not put upon, Eli prayed. *That this beast shall not turn his back from the sword. Upon him rattle the quiver, the flashing knives, and the rifle. Deliver it unto me, safe and comforted in your infernal and holiest names.*

One looked into the eyes of the other; man and beast shared mournful understanding. Eli backed away. He mouthed apologies, whispered condolences.

The Baldknobbers hollered over who was next to climb the hill. They argued the point of who among them was best suited to tend to their fallen leader: Him who sobbed in the brush.

I shall burn for this. He cursed the star above which would not sleep. *If not at the hand of mine Gods, then surely set aflame by the tortured Earth itself.*

He turned heel and ran.

The mule watched him go.

Eli sprinted through the forest in a serpentine until his

lungs wore out and his side ached. He could hear, from time to time, a stray shout or command from the Baldknobbers behind him. The pounding of hooves on limestone and shale spurred him on and he took no rest. As the hours wore on, the sound of rushing blood filled him from temple to brain and he heard no more.

What kin am I to the deaf adder that stoppeth his own ear?

In the silence of exhaustion, Eli's mind returned to the preceding moments of these calamitous events:

Bull Walker, in his Devil's mask, at the door to Eli's cabin. A map is required of Eli, warlock for hire. Contracts are signed. One in ink, another in blood. A sack of coin is exchanged.

Take us to the stump, *the Baldknobbers demand– those masked and gruesome bringers of vigilante justice.* A place of power and will, we seek.

Bring me a bird of peace, *Eli answers,* that I may offer its feathers to the Gods and be shown the way.

Eli, now at the altar of granite, strangles a heron upon the stone. The sun of Earth falls beneath the hillside– like pennies down the well –and is replaced by a doppelganger star where should hang the lunar equalizer of shore and space and the passing of time.

Accusations are leveled: Where is the map? Is he drunk? *They shout and scream:* Has he done it right? Where goes the darkness? Why only sun? *They point their guns and juggle their knives. Masks are pulled over hard faces.*

Eli mounts his mule and he rides. He shoots. He runs.

The sun will not die.

The moon cannot rise.

And still they call out to him: What will God say? *And:* What have you done?

Glimpses of these mistakes and misfortunes cloistered his thoughts as he ran. Faster than his racing mind. Further than he had deemed possible for a man of his physicality. The foreign sun tracked his every move with misplaced shadow and hollow rays of heat. He sweated and wept but did not cease. Until– upon end of what should have been his second day of the chase– Eli arrived at the stump.

Though he had only heard tell of it in occulted texts and passing conversation with fellow men and women of his order, places of magical renown were not unfamiliar to him. He had, for instance, laid hands on an anvil from south of the border which was said to consume souls. Eli had also once traveled to a township where nameless musicians played handmade instruments in a ritualistic attempt to summon the void. None of which sated his interest in full– only offered cloudy visions of the strangeness which cloaks our world.

Nor had these encounters prepared him for the quiet malevolence of the stump: Unlike past dalliances with strange folk in eldritch lands, Eli felt a twinge of terror standing before the black and twisted remnants of the dead oak. Subtle in its unpleasantries, the stump was as plain as it was upending. It seethed with complacency.

Eli's general unease shifted to terror upon realization that the surrounding forest had simply ceased to be. An endless sea of depressed growth with nary a tree to behold. Had Eli not combed the thick bosom of the forest for hours? If not a day–? And yet all was reduced to dead grasses as far as the eye could see. Save of course, the cleaved remnants of the smoldering oak.

Gone too– and perhaps more disarming– was the wretched sun that haunted Eli for the sin of casting his spell. The moon reigned once more and stars freckled the radiance of her lunar majesty– though the passing of cycles was but a snapshot. There had been no order to the cosmic changing of the guard. No glowing fall or stoic rise. Only a cruel equivalency. The summation of time through the misunderstanding of an extraterrestrial God.

And if mine heavenly Father prepareth a place for me, He

*will return and taketh me to be with Him that I also may be
where He lay dreaming.*

Eli dropped to his knees at the base of the stump where
black roots jabbed the soil. Charred and veined like burned
yams beneath strips of ebon bark, he observed obscene undu-
lations that marked their subterranean passage. As if its radi-
cles suckled on the loam.

*There is a stump whose roots are as tongues, and its tubers as
teeth, to devour the life from off the earth.*

He removed his hat and set the shotgun aside. The earth
wobbled. His head swam. He sought to gain purchase and
grabbed at the ground: A membranous mass which housed
unfathomable fluids beneath the surface of its grassy skin.
Fingers plunged through clay. Eli wished to scream as his head
slid inside the earth. A rapturous quiver sucked his breath
away. An alarming orgasm buckled his knees as luxurious dirt
filled his open mouth. Arms and shoulders disappeared.

*Behold: The veil betwixt two temples torn in twain. The
earth shivers and stones are split. Widen the mysterious chasms
of the cosmos until His Grand Emptiness hath been revealed
to me.*

Eli swam through a starless void. His clothing had been
shorn from his body, though he could not recall when or how
this had come to pass. Velvet darkness slicked against flesh as if
he were being shuttled through a womb. Perception of sight
returned to him, and tentacles of deeper black descended from
above– roots that rippled with life. The scorched tendrils
enveloped him, caressed him with rutted bark. Scratched him.
Nibbled.

A circle of flickering orange appeared overhead from
within the tomb of tubers. Eli gasped, soundless, at the churning, hallowed flames. Warmth flitted through the glassy nothing. He was lifted higher into the black folds, towards the halo
of Hell, until his scalp crested its ring. His head, he realized,
had entered the interior of the stump.

Consumed, he thought, *mine skull, the burnt offering.*

Eli's eyes slid past the circle and it banded across them like a visor. For a moment, he saw only fire, and thought he would surely perish. Then the visions came:

The wood of the stump that was once a tree. And the stones and the dust that nestled in its roots. Come hither! Lap at black water in the trenches of her bark. Vestige of dark will, this supple Autumn oak. A robed mystic sits in her boughs: He who hath given heed to seducing spirits, and doctrines of devils.

For the passage of one hundred moons, the mystic studies the shape of the earth in the confines of her branches. Though many false prophets are gone out into the world, he is of an order all his own. He speaketh expressly to passersby, that in the latter times some shall depart from the faith of one God, and be welcomed to his vision of duality. His bearded mouth whispers of communal spells and occulted works that will bring forth a merging of the Lord God, above, and His Infernal Majesty, below. This melding of Darkness and Light will etch a new reign of worldly pleasures, he assures them.

Do not let treacherous talk spill from your throats, *he warns the gathering crowds.* Speak only what may benefit those who listen. Those who consider themselves religious do not keep a tight rein on their tongues. They deceive themselves, and their faith is worthless.

It is not long before the onlookers and casual listeners betray their promise. They soon return to their townships, where they bring news to their families and leaders. Word spreads of the mystic in the tree. His blasphemous teachings reach the churches and lawmen. Posses are formed. Knives are sharpened. Torches are lit.

You misunderstand, *the mystic tells a group of usurpers, gathered beneath the tree.* I too serveth the Lord God on high. I also fear Lucifer the Morning Star. I am but a humble hermit. I tremble and worship. I keep the sacred oaths. And yet, my brethren, I see a path of light through darkness.

They listen, and though they are uneasy, they wait.

We are, all of us, children of God. But does thy God not also teach that the entirety of Earth be under thy Dark Lord's control? Does thou not repay evil with blessing so that thou may inherit a blessing? Woe to those who misinterpret sweet for bitter. For Satan does not delight in love, but instead rejoices with truth, *he preaches.*

The first stone is cast and blood is spilled from the mystic's head. Casks of holy oils are emptied on the Oak. They point their torches, beg forgiveness, and set the tree ablaze. The mystic burns among the branches, speaks sweetly all the while. His skin drizzles down from above to shrivel and coil at their feet. Within the hour, only a blackened skeleton   remains, and it yammers endlessly with chattering teeth. The fire rages on and on but the sun refuses to rise. Darkness and smoke.

Concern takes hold: Has God punished them? Have they angered something else? Something older–?

Those who attempt to flee find themselves unable to locate their homes. They return within a matter of moments to the flaming tree, as if they ran in circles– as if the dark night were a tide, pushing them back a mile for every forward stroke.

Madness takes them. Those who could no longer bear the muttering bones of a man who should be dead began to hurl themselves into the bon. Their bodies melt and they fuse together with root and bark and chattering bones.

The remaining townsfolk take up their axes and picks. They swing and hack wildly through the blaze, until many more are dead, and at last the Oak falls.

As it does, the sun returns.

It rises over the smoking stump, warms their blistered flesh, and all is as the Lord God intended; Satan watches from below, keeps the moon close to their bosom, and waits.

Eli saw all of this, watched it like a dream. Other, ancient dramas also played before his eyes: The shape of the cosmos before God or Satan came to be. A slithering creature that swayed among the stars, took root in the dust of creation, and called itself the Oak. These histories were hard to absorb– difficult to parse in their vast strangeness. It troubled him greatly, yet he could not look away in the confines of the barken cocoon.

All the while, Eli's body changed beneath the earth.

The Bald Knobbers– what was left of them –kicked at the stump and scratched their hooded heads. A gopher hole at its base was all that remained of their quarry– the hole, and the sudden passage of the moon, which they assumed had been the warlock's doing.

Their horses milled about and chomped on wet fronds. Eli's mule tarried behind them, whined softly, and did not eat.

Bull Walker sat in the grass and stared at the fading stars with teeth bared. A thick hatred coated the chambers of his heart. His lungs rattled with each sucking breath and he knew that soon he would be dead.

One of his men spread his knees beside him and spat. "What say?"

"We ain't leaving til we've found him," Bull replied.

The Bald Knobber regarded the hole and spat again. The tassels on his horns were damp with fog and early morning air. He scratched at his face beneath the mask.

"He's nearby," Bull said. His eyes were glassy and brimmed with distant, burning suns. "I can smell him."

"Seems like maybe he ain't, what with night falling. Figure maybe he's been took care of. I'd say we got lucky, Bull. The boys reckon we ought call it. Get you back to the Doc."

"Like Hell," Bull tried to rise but there was a sharp snap along his ribs and he stayed where he sat. "We got to find him. We was so close. We could have it all. Don't you understand? Don't you see what that *thing* is–?" Bull crooked a finger at the stump. "Do you know what it can do?"

The Bald Knobber shook his head. "All I know is we got one dead man– a good man –and another on the way."

Bull wheezed.

"I see a hole big enough for a critter, a dead tree, and the moon." The Bald Knobber rose and dusted his shins. "That's enough for me, Bull."

"I can't ride," Bull wiped dew from his brow.

"Well."

"I won't leave. I can't. What'll I do? Will you sorry bastards leave me behind? That your aim?"

The masked man moved away from him. He wandered back to the other Bald Knobbers, looked over his shoulder, and said: "We'll leave you the mule."

"You fools! Curs of your mother's curdled cunts."

"Hope you find your way back to us, Bull. We surely do."

When his men had crested a hill– left him alone– Bull Walker began his attempt to coax the mule. He smacked the ground, and whistled– even offered it a sullen lullaby– but the beast would not return so much as a glance. Curses were hurled next: Fiendish threats of violence. He ran his throat red from where he sat, and when these attempts failed, Bull pleaded and sobbed for it to come. He denied himself any further attempts to stand, knowing full well that he could not.

When at last he went quiet, and the tears had frozen to his whiskers, the earth itself began to move. Slow at first, it lapped like waves at the base of the black stump, and shuttled Bull Walker's buttocks across the crumbling crusts– dragged him ever closer to the apparent source of vibration. The hole beside the stump widened, sucked in loose gravel and jittering dirt. The Bald Knobber– soon to be swallowed up by the hole, had silently resigned himself to a fate of unknown depths.

Before his boots had reached the precipice, Bull was thrown backwards by a dark form which burst through the ground. He somersaulted– head over ass– and felt the bones of his back slice against his ruined ribcage.

The mule shied off a few paces and stopped. Quick bursts of frigid air plumed from its wide nostrils. It watched these events unfold with black, marble eyes that reflected the tittering star.

Bull Walker screamed but the air had been taken from him and so was mostly quiet in his pain. Above his twisted body, the towering figure swayed– a black tree of gnarled branches and ebon skin. The tree shook, though there was no wind, and dust lifted from its naked limbs to swirl like cyclones through the sky. The Bald Knobber flopped onto his side. He looked upon the tree with fear and followed the base of what was once the stump with his eyes until they met another's. In the center of the trunk, there was a face. The face of a man set in wood, with radiant eyes so familiar, and yet wholly obscene.

Again, Bull shouted, and again, could not form a sound beyond a gasping, raspy whisper.

Eli the Tree did not care if the Bald Knobber recognized him in his new body– this prison. Such simple thoughts as vengeance and comeuppance were beneath him. That his enemy should suffer in darkness or be shown the light of mercy was of no consequence. He had transcended to a new realm of understanding and so did nothing but stare upon the slow death of his former employer with the tranquil gaze of a God.

Hear mine voice from mine barken temple: May the earth shake and tremble; that the foundations of the hills may also quake and churn. For once I was angry, and smoke went up from mine nostrils, and thou devoured the fire from mine mouth; I bowed the heavens also, and came down with darkness under mine roots. And I rode upon a seed, and grew; I grew upon the soul of the Earth, and made darkness mine secret place; mine canopy around me was dark branches, and thick leaves bent to mine skies.

The hours passed, slow and cold, until the new dawn broke in its entirety over the hills. Warmth flicked away the infantile jags of frost upon the grass, and remnant drops of dew expired along the corpse of Bull Walker. Golden rays sliced open the stars and ripped all memory of the great white orb from her lunar seat.

In the morning sun, the surrounding forest reappeared as if it had never ceased to be.

The mule ate a breakfast of sweet hillside ferns, and edged closer to the Tree that was its master. Once beneath his branches, Eli the Tree called to it, and a sound like creaking timber escaped his crooked mouth. The beast was startled and shied away. Eli the Tree spoke again– bent his mighty limbs to stroke its head– but the mule brayed and ran from him; bounded through the forest, up and over a squat knoll.

Eli the Tree watched the mule go. He saw it stop, once, and turn to look back at him. It kicked out at nothing and took off again– was followed by whirls of dust and seed until it was gone.

Sadness– the last emotion he would ever be allowed to feel– gripped his oaken chest with a fierceness that made the branches of his head sway and groan. He tipped back his jagged lips, and a hollow moan fluted from the deepest funnels of his bark covered lungs.

After a while, Eli The Tree closed his pendulous lids and waited for lightning to strike.

Oh, Earth, he prayed. *Burn away mine deeds until all is ash. Strip me of the horrors. Release me from this fate.*

"Now tell me," the Goddess said, "what have you learn't?"

"I'm not sure," he replied.

The Goddess of the wood laughed at him. "Then there ain't nothing I can do for ye," she said, "and all bad dogs go to market. Dig up that saw, and let's get on with it."

He sank into the wrinkles of her belly.

XX.

QUEEN OF THE GIMPS

JACK PACE PISSED INTO HIS BUCKET WHILE A wealthy Field Pirate watched him through the bars. He shook himself dry, as if he were alone, and sank back into a corner of the cage. The once fearsome warrior hugged his knees and folded into a ball.

Morning having only just arrived, the mercenary stockade was mostly empty: The proprietor of the camp spoke with potential customers– a sparse crowd of early birds who milled about the rows of cages– and helped them to appraise the wares within.

"Don't look like no Chaindevil to me," the pirate said, and sucked on his wooden teeth. "Ain't look like much of anything."

The Merc-Dealer– engaged in a sale with a merchant from the West Plains Battalion– politely excused herself and sidled up to the pirate. "He might be worse for wear," she told him, "but this here's the real deal."

"Uh-huh."

"You ever go up against a 'Devil? You hear what come of them mutants out in Briarwood? Nasty stuff. A steal at this price."

"Where'd you say y'all found him?"

"The Crone brung him up out the holler just 'fore dawn. You should've seen him: Took an hour to get him off her tit. Calling her the 'Goddess,' and all. I like to have never seen such a thing. You hear stories: How they been whipped to worship one such as me–" she gestured to herself, tracing lines down her body– "and how them Bald Knobbers is the only men what could keep our friend here at bay... And baby, call me a believer, 'cus this sum'bastard won't so much as look me in the eye. Reckon he'd strangle your cock from its socket if I was to open up that cage."

The Field Pirate dabbed at a river of sweat that ran from his hat brim.

"Anyhow," she continued, "that ol' woman salvaged me a keeper. Even brung back his chainsaw. Witches ain't good for much, but she sure done me a favor; nearly dragged his ass back from the grave, tell you what."

"Looks to me like he ain't quite come out of it."

"Well he ain't been fed nothing but titty milk. Ain't had no dope in God knows how long. You know how they are: Red eyed or dead in a ditch. Not much in-between for a beast like'at."

"Starved or not, he won't last long once word gets out. I got plenty of takers."

"Including the ones what own him, I reckon." The pirate turned away from the cage. "Her Majesty don't take kindly to man-thieving. Ain't enough cannons on all my schooners could keep them Ozarkians off our ass if'n they come to reclaim him."

The Merc-Dealer chuckled. "Her Majesty can't do shit. Ain't you heard?"

The Field Pirate scrunched his brow.

"Chief Commando Larson and his Kansas fuck-o's crossed the border last night. Ozarkians got their hands full. You say you're headed for Oklahoma? Can't imagine no River

94

Maidens wading that far out for a cast-off like this'n here." She kicked the cage with a copper-tipped boot.

Jack rocked on the dirt floor, and muttered softly.

"Well," the pirate said, "he'll take some work. What say you take a mule-boy off the price, and maybe we'll–"

"Greetings, Petunia."

The Merc-Dealer spun on her heels.

Three women approached her as they strolled past the rows of cages: Two carried silver pitchforks and wore pointed, bird-like helmets of cast-iron, while the third was dressed in a lavish shawl of emu feathers and bull snake scales. The pits of her eyes had been painted with coal, and each tip of her lashes was adorned with a small green gem. In her pearl-studded gauntlet, she held a leash of dark silk on which a man in red leather was tethered. The leashed man took short, stomping steps, with the backs of his covered wrists held to his breast: An exaggerated display of supplication. The bright leather that covered his face was seamless, save for a hole around the mouth.

"We've come to see the Chaindevil," the woman said, and pulled at the leash. Her charge gagged, then halted. He fell to her bare feet, and turned over on his back. One of the guards stooped to one knee to rub his smooth, red belly.

"Hail, Madam Beech," the Merc-Dealer said. She turned to the Field Pirate, and shoved him away from the cage. "Sale's over," she said.

Madam Beech yanked the leash, harder this time, and the leather man retched. Her guard grunted beneath her helm, rose, and slapped him across the buttocks as he scrambled to his feet.

"Right this way," the Merc-Dealer said. She spread her arms in offering; bowed to Jack Pace where he cowered behind bars.

The Field Pirate produced a pipe of black cob, lighted it with his ring-strike, and glared at the group of women. "Dirty, damn shame to keep a 'Devil in bondage," he said. "I'll put three extra mule-boys on top of the price."

The guards strode forward in silence; they leveled their pitchforks at the pirate in tandem.

"Get gone," Madam Beech said, "and I won't relieve you of your mules– Hell, *everything* you own."

The Field Pirate put his hands up and walked backwards. "Fair enough," he said between the pipe-stem. "'S'all yours."

With a sharp snap of iron, Madam Beech's guards halted, and jammed their weapons into soil. They crossed their arms in defensive posture, and watched the pirate's retreat.

"Say, Petunia," the Field Pirate called back, "we still on for dinner?"

"Keep moving, id'jit," the Merc-Dealer answered.

"A goddamned shame," he said. The Field Pirate whistled, rounded the stalls, and was gone.

"Awful sorry about that," the Merc-Dealer said.

Madam Beech nodded, a slight smile trickled down the edge of her painted mouth.

"Right this way."

The leather man scampered forward, and Madam Beech passed his leash to one of her guards. He went down on his knees beside their armored toes– whined for scratches. The guards ignored him.

Once she had made her way to the front of his cage, Madam Beech snapped her fingers at Jack. She mewled through the bars– a cloying sound of hunger– until the Chaindevil peeled his arms from his face to look upon her. "Hidy," she said.

Jack pushed himself upright, wedged his back against a wall coated in wads of coagulated fluid. He breathed hard and fast; reached for his vacant chainsaw like the ghost of a severed limb.

Madam Beech removed her shawl. She touched her naked body, felt the warmth of the sun, and let her gaze drift away from the cage. A yawn escaped her lips as she stretched for the sky– legs spread, an un-dashed asterisk of flesh and hair.

Jack closed his eyes.

The Merc-Dealer watched, nervous, and prayed for the sale.

A few moments passed, and when she was satisfied, Madam Beech reclaimed her shawl– pulled it tight across her shoulders. "Well then," she said, "I do believe we can salvage this'n. Seems like the break has kept." She looked at Jack– "That so? Is you a good doggy? Think you can keep to the Old Ways? I'll bet you will. Gonna look mighty handsome in your new leather britches." She held her hand behind her back, snapped her fingers twice.

The guard to her left unsheathed the pitchfork from the earth. She turned her helm downard, raised the weapon, and jammed it at the man in red leather. The silver prongs sank into his skull with a click. He collapsed to his stomach, and she pushed her boot against the back of his masked head. The guard pulled back, and her pitchfork came free.

"I got his saw," the Merc-Dealer said. "If'n you want it."

"That won't be necessary," Madam Beech replied. She stared at Jack– her eyes like emerald fire. "Will it?"

XXI.

ON WAVES OF GRASS

THE FIELD SHIP OF MADAM BEECH WAS THE LARGEST vessel Jack Pace had ever seen, let alone ridden upon: A brutalist rectangle of dark steel and canvas tread– the vastness of which made him quiver in his leather jumpsuit.

The red leathers were comfortably tight and seasonally warm, though he wished his predecessor's mask had not been destroyed by the pitchfork– would rather have stood beneath the ship in blindness. It rumbled to life upon their approach, and shook the ground beneath them. Twin pipes of heat-lacerated copper burped out clouds of yellow bio-diesel: Jack smelled the remnants of men without names and wondered just how many bodies it took to run an engine the size of a Bald Knob church house– asked himself how long it would be before he joined them in its furnace.

They boarded the Field Ship with both guards carrying the shaven, naked corpse between them. Madam Beech held the former Chaindevil on his leash.

It was there, in the cherry-wood furnishings of the ship's containment quarters, that Jack learned the pleasures of unobstructed oppression– both of the body, as well as his mind.

He began each day by waking at the foot of Madam

Beech's bed. There, the sun would warm his face through the port-hole, and he clambered from his nest of beaded pillows to scratch at the door. Madam Beech, too, rose at dawn's first light: She wrapped herself in robes, locked his leash into place, and walked him to the deck. Side-by-side, the two of them would squat over the railing, and do their morning business. Jack would first wipe the Madam, and then himself. From then on, it was to the chambers for food or wine, whoopings, lubricant, and tears of joyous agony. There were intermittent breaks for smoking– more strolls upon the deck– as well as occasional meetings in the war-room where Madam Beech would give orders to the crew while Jack lay beside her. After these brief respites came the studded paddles– the chains, and crosses– until supper and sleep.

Oh, sleep, he often thought, *how I've missed you.*

Much like the nameless fool who had been speared through his skull at the mercenary camp, Jack witnessed the deaths of many man-pets on the Field Ship. It was difficult to parse when or how they were selected for sacrifice, but as he first suspected, the corpses were indeed heaved into the furnace which fueled the great ship. His time would come when it came. Nothing to do, nothing to say.

"Me?" The old man's voice came to him, as it often did when he pondered his eventual outcome: *"I simply cannot wait for the day..."*

But die by the Madam's hand, he did not, and until the eve of Halloween, Jack Pace found peace in the chains of her will.

XXII.
RETURN THE DOG

MADAM BEECH WALKED HER MAN-PET DOWN THE ramp and onto Ozarkian soil. Before them, a river of filth cleaved a delicate, shimmering band across the field. Across the water, smoke lilted from behind a dark wall to mingle with the clouds above. The air smelled of cinnamon and dirty water– a stomach churning swell of savory sweets. She lingered beside the Field Ship with a long, thin joint between her fingers. Four guards flanked her at each corner with their pitchforks held at the waist, but still, she was nervous.

Leash slack, subordinate in posture, Jack stayed close to his Madam. He watched a pack of bionic buzzards wheel overhead; they clacked and screeched– sent signals to each other, and to the township beyond the wall. Surrounded by trees he once called brothers, rocks that had been his bed– familiar sights and sounds all around him– Jack heaved from a seesaw of emotions. He swallowed back the bile of raw, bloody memories.

Home, he knew: The last place he ever hoped to see.

As the aluminum gilded buzzards returned to their roosts– sailing noisily through October's last light– a line of figures appeared on the horizon. They moved forward, knee-deep in water, and their form coalesced: The River Maidens, dreaded assassins of Her Majesty, stood arm in arm with weighted razor-nets tied to the hems of blue skirts. Tridents and spears were strapped to their tight, tanned backs. Each body shorn of its hair, their skulls bloomed purple in reflection of their aquatic hunting grounds.

"Avast," they said from afar, though Madam Beech and her attendants had not moved.

"All hail Her Majesty of the Ozarks," the Madam replied, hand to her mouth.

"Take heed," the River Maidens said. "Turn heel, and be well."

"Hear me," she answered. "I come with a gift."

Jack wetted himself. The stench of wine-heavy urine escaped the neckband of his leathers. Nostrils assaulted by the odor, he belched and gagged– tried to be still.

The River Maidens bent their ranks to form an ouroboros, and though their legs traversed the river, they made not so much as a splash nor left a single gurgle in their wake. The crescent shape of interwoven warriors descended upon itself until the line became a circle. The Maidens bowed their bald heads in conversation. They spoke in stoic tones and hushed murmurs– none of which echoed back to the Madam and her trembling gimp.

In a sudden flurry of movement, the River Maidens spun and flung themselves across the bank. A stampede of swift feet and cunning eyes. Nets were unlatched to be twirled like lassos over their heads; spears spun out from behind them, gripped by wrinkled, briny hands. They crossed the grass with increasing speed– bounded towards the Field Ship.

Madam Beech's guards braced their knees, and brandished the silver pitchforks– jabbed them in defense.

"At ease," the Madam ordered. "Drop them forks on the ground."

The guards did as they were told, and the Maidens

stopped just short of the ship. Dirt skidded up from their bare feet in tidy plumes: A gust of forced wind and heavy breathing that sent the feathers of Madam Beech's shawl aflutter.

The Madam bowed without hesitation and said: "This is yours." She dropped Jack's leash.

The Maidens bore down on the man who cowered between her legs– tore the red leather jumpsuit from his twisted frame– and lifted him, naked, onto their shoulders. They turned from the Madam and her guards without a word, and began to carry him away.

"For my troubles," Madam Beech said, caution on her tongue, "I'd tarry Her Majesty's patience for a boon."

A single Maiden broke from the group. She stalked back to the ship with agitated steps, and a dark look set in her face. "Well," she said, "spit it out, bitch."

"We're bound for the Northern kingdoms," Madam Beech replied. "I seek safe passage through Her Majesty's border. Will y'all grant it?"

"Get on," the River Maiden said. "Make it quick."

She spun on waterlogged heels and stormed back to join the fold of her sisters.

The Madam called after her: "What about Larson? We heard the Kansas Front come through– is it safe?"

The River Maiden laughed. She regrouped as they stormed across the river, and muttered something to the others. Their heads tilted forward and back– green teeth clicked and clacked. They all laughed.

XXIII.

THE HALLOWEEN PARADE

JACK PACE SAT ON THE GROUND WITH HANDS tethered to his feet by a length of twine. He had been placed there– nude and wet– in the shadow of the wall. Not a clue as to his fate, for the River Maidens had said nothing to him, and promptly returned to their post once he was hogtied.

Hour upon hour he waited, until at last– just before sunset– the Courier came to take him away.

"Well, howdy-doo," she said. "How you been, Jack?"

He was quiet– stared down at his tangled mass of beard, and absently noted how much longer– and lighter– it had grown. His gnarled wrists, the length and looseness of his grayish member by way of gravity and age, and a stuttering heart that never seemed to slow: It felt as though he had lived one hundred lives, all in a month's time.

And time, he remembered, *she's the Reaper...*

"Now let's see here: Counting your previous offenses– adding the murder of not one, but *two* Bald Knobbers... Plus God knows how many of your own along the way... Multiplied by the uncon'ch'able act of desertion... Hoo-wee!" The Courier wiped the brow of her helm in mockery of his shame. "That's quite a total you got there. Gonna guess we're somewhere around sixty-nine-deductions-and-your-dead-fuckin-ass."

Jack Pace smiled. His last true smile.

"Lucky for you," she said, "they's been some changes 'round here: Ain't no more Chaindevils. Y'all got the Royal pink-slip– what's left of ye, anyhow."

Jack was confused, and his head pained him.

"Only twenty of you cum'shooters come back from the shit– empty-handed, I ought to add– and when Larson and his Kansans stormed through two weeks back, I reckon y'all dropped down to five. Six, if'n you count the dog. Which I do. He's sight better at killing than you lot ever was. Don't go around eating his own, neither. He's a good'n, that ol' hound. Formed us a new guard around him– got El Cazador running the show these days. Got him running patrol on the southern border. They make quite the pair, him and that beast. We hope to breed some pups come springtime– can't imagine we'll find a bitch of his size, mind you, but we'll do our damndest."

The sun hung low, and had turned the color of cinnamon cider. A hazy, drooped orb– the last gulp of a steaming mug.

"Yessir," the Courier slapped her ironclad thigh, "I'd say it's all working out dandy. No chainsaws to motor sure saves us a load of grease."

"What about Larson?" Jack asked.

"River Maidens cleaned up after your dead pals– wiped Chief Commando off the face o' the Earth. Got his head on a stick out by your old stomping grounds. And to that, I'll say this: Ain't quite the same without the Field o' Pain. Her Majesty had it burned out. Smoke so thick you could damn near taste the popping-corn. No need for mazes, I suppose. But, boy, did I love to sit up on that wall and watch them kids come through. Y'all knew how to spook a field mouse, I'll grant ye that much."

Pride welled up along the rusted rivets of his heart. All he had ever wanted to hear, and there it was: Finally spoken, fully heard.

It made him sick.

"If it's all over– if we ain't needed no more– what would Her Majesty have me do?" Jack held back the tears that so desperately needed to run. "Where will I go?"

"That's for me to know," the Courier said, "and you to light upon." She unhooked a serrated dirk from her side, and slashed open his binds. "Let's go."

They walked along the wall for what felt to Jack an eternity. A death march: Him exposed, unaware, and with a pump-slugger aimed at his back; her giggling with cruelty at his broken gait, his bleeding heels.

Night fell across the land, and voices cried out within the wall. A glow erupted in its interior– a mighty orange hue that flickered and cast strange shadows on the hillsides beyond. The stench of sugared squash and beer-lathered meats beckoned to Jack and the Courier. They rounded a corner and came upon an open gate where burning light framed a square upon the grass.

Jack halted before the entry, and turned to face the Courier.

"Go on," she said. "Get!"

On legs of quaking flesh and bone, he did as he was told. Jack ambled through the gate, into the fire.

"Here he walks along a country road,
An' with him, our hearts journey too."

The song leapt out at him on all sides: A chorus of folk who sang with earnest mouths and loving tones.

"Bent low beneath the burden of his load
Was a 'Devil, a 'Devil I knew.
Held high above the stump of his head

Was Her Majesty's grace to be earned."

A mass of women huddled together with their men and their children in tow. They wore handsome, plaid linen with ornamental buttons of brass– well-kept slacks, oiled shoes. Swords tied to the waist of every sister; round, happy babies to the breast of every man at their side.

All together, they sang:

"He has walked along a country road,
An' with him, our hearts journeyed too."
Put down thy saw, and follow me
I have heard Her Majesty's call.
How can he make greater sacrifice
When our Chaindevil gave us his all."

Jack Pace stood naked before them on a street cobbled by pond pebbles and smooth crystal. The road glittered by the light of two A-frame bonfires that raged on either side. Squat structures of timber and glass flanked the street with gated outcroppings that stretched away from open doors, and where airborne benches tied with chain swung from the eaves.

Gutted pumpkins and turnips with smiling, ghastly faces lined the street. They stared out from windows– sat in the branches of trees– and flickered with the red warmth of their intestinal candles.

"What is this?" Jack asked.

"It's all for you," the Courier replied. She walked back the way she had come, and shut the gate behind her.

The Ozarkian townsfolk began to circle, took up their song once more, and surrounded him. They were beautiful– healthy and clean. Their breath reeked of sobriety. They watched him with fine-tipped pupils like the whittled points of blackened sticks. The town, too, was pristine– well ordered, easy on the eyes. A living entity: Fat from food, comfort, and the humble nature of those who dwelled in its belly.

Jack had drifted away by the spell of their song, closed his eyes to better feel it, and so did not see the Bald Knob cultists: A line of horns and masks. Charred teeth set to rictus lips. Filthy fingers clutched candle-bearing squash. One hundred swerving blades.

The music stopped, and Jack Pace opened his eyes. The Ozarkians had returned to their homes. They shut their doors, snuffed out their lights, and turned their backs to him. In their place, the Bald Knobbers now stood.

"Bristol?"

The Bald Knobber in front of him said nothing. Green sweat bubbled down its lip. It blinked with slow, cross-eyed stupidity.

"Were you Bristol? Prancer? Marsha?"

From behind, a pair of the cultists draped a gray cloak across his bare body; helped slip his arms through the sleeves; tied the sash across his waist; secured the twisted buck knife.

"Baby? Baby Stuey, that you? Do I know you? Ruby–? Ol' Ruby, do you remember me?"

"I do," the Bald Knobber said, and pulled the mask over Jack's head.

ACKNOWLEDGMENTS

To those who stayed up late and watched me howl these pages
into a shitty microphone-
To the readers who loaned out their eyes; sliced the throats of
their precious time-
To the Gods of Craft who heard me scratching, opened their
doors-
To the family who kept me-
To the one who loved me-
To Mother Cannabis-
To Missouri-
From the bottom of my heart, thank you. Thank you for
everything.

Obliged, eternal.

-Matthew Mitchell

ABOUT THE AUTHOR

Matthew Mitchell is a fiction and comics writer from the Missouri Ozarks. His short stories can be found in the Black Metal Horror anthologies from Castaigne Publishing. He is co-creator of the Horrorium comic series, and his work has appeared in Heavy Metal Magazine. Matthew currently lives in Kansas City with his lovely partner and their cat.

ALSO FROM WEIRDPUNK BOOKS

What is happening to Katherine?

Someone put something into her at the plasma center and took it back out again. By the time her friends catch up to her, she's not exactly the person they remember. She has begun to change into something new, and if they're going to help her escape the people who did this to her, they may need to transform, too.

Squarely in both the crime and body horror traditions, Mutant Circuit reads like Elmore Leonard and David Cronenberg meeting at 3 AM in a run-down strip-mall parking lot, and Mark Jaskowski is the conspirator who brought them there.

"Jaskowski wields words like weapons, his prose quick and sharp as a butterfly knife. The result: a truly original work in the corpus of body horror." – Brendan Vidito (*Pornography for the End of the World, Nightmares in Ecstasy*)

A Small Light & Other Stories - Sara Century

A mysterious woman stalks a seaside town. An isolated couple inhabit a house full of tropical birds. A rowboat floats down a river toward a witch's cave. Death wanders an unnamed city during the plague. Sara Century's debut short story collection carries with it surreal visions inspired by pulp paperbacks, art house films, comic books of all flavors, and classic queer villains. A Small Light & Other Stories gathers tales that hinge on troubled characters with nothing left to lose encountering existential horrors, where everyday problems escalate into insurmountable monsters, and we find ourselves unable to escape dreams long since transformed into nightmares.

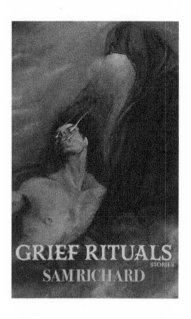

Grief Rituals - Sam Richard

From Wonderland Award-Winning author Sam Richard comes twelve more uncomfortable tales of sorrow, ruination, and transformation.

A young widow joins a spousal loss support group with bizarre methods of healing. An aging punk is stalked by something ancient and familiar in the labyrinthian halls of an art complex. A couple renting out a small movie theater are interrupted by a corrosive force of nature. Through these stories of weird horror and visceral sorrow, Richard shows us ways grief can be transcendent—but only if we know which rituals to practice.

Made in the USA
Las Vegas, NV
21 September 2024

95592262R00080